Three Nights in December

C. Chérie Hardy

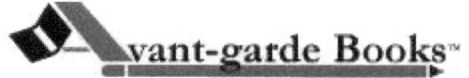

Fiction Division
Post Office Box 566
Mableton, Georgia 30126
www.avantgardebooks.net

Three Nights in December

Book Cover Graphics: Suzanne Horwitz

ISBN: 978-0-9908992-0-4

Manufactured in the United States of America

This book is dedicated to:

Larmetria Trammell
and
Yolanda Wilfork

Larmetria,
You said you were looking for something good to read. I promised you I'd write something for you; I sincerely hope that this book will do.

Yolanda,
You once said that there was a "novel in me". Well, this is the first, but I pray not the last. Thank you for your encouragement!

"To everything there is a season, and a time to every purpose under the heaven: a time to be born, and a time to die; a time to plant, and a time to pluck up that which is planted; a time to kill, and a time to heal; a time to break down, and a time to build up; a time to weep, and a time to laugh; a time to mourn, and a time to dance; a time to cast away stones, and a time to gather stones together; a time to embrace, and a time to refrain from embracing; a time to get, and a time to lose; a time to keep, and a time to cast away; a time to rend, and a time to sew; a time to keep silence, and a time to speak; a time to love, and a time to hate; a time of war, and a time of peace."

–Ecclesiastes 3:1-7 (KJV)

Three Nights in December
Table of Contents
C. Chérie Hardy

Table of Contents
Three Nights in December
C. Chérie Hardy

Three Nights in December

Chapter 1
The Verdict

"We, the jury, find the defendant, Kaseem Jones, to be 'not guilty' of the charge of second degree murder."

Not guilty. The words pierced through Netar's mind like thunder so loudly that he momentarily became deaf. In shock, he slowly rose from his seat. His blood had jolted from ninety-eight degrees to boiling point before he could blink. He vaguely recognized his mother's voice a few feet away sobbing uncontrollably while the judge fiercely pounded his gavel against the sounding block.

"Order!" he shouted.

"Order in the court!" the judge repeated.

With the second blast of the gavel restoring Netar's hearing, his eyes jetted from his weeping mother, who was being comforted by his father and brother, to the defendant who greeted him with a maniacal sneer. As Netar's eyes blazed into his nemesis, Kaseem Jones seemed to transfigure into something unrecognizable — something nonhuman. His teeth became fang-like and his skin switched to a light gray with scales.

C. Chérie Hardy

While the officers watched both men warily, Netar's and Kaseem's eyes dueled and smoldered with wild rage. Netar took a step forward. And, so did the beast. The officers, expecting the worse, rushed closer with their guns drawn. But Netar, remembering his father's words as a child, quickly lifted his hands in the air and slowly pivoted to indicate that he was leaving the room. He heard a small voice telling him that if he didn't immediately vacate the premises, he would bring more heartache to his grieving mother.

With his love for her guiding him, Netar managed to resist the impulse to fight and destroy his sister's killer for a few seconds before quietly abandoning the emotional pandemonium inside and around him.

As he exited the courthouse, the heat quickly sobered his bloodthirsty heart. Instantaneously, his body became drenched with sweat. He loosened his tie and was tempted to remove his jacket but decided to leave it on despite feeling like he had just entered a sauna. His father had insisted on him wearing a suit to the trial although he felt he was overdressed for the occasion.

"People often act the way they dress,"

he'd often say to him and his brother. "Wearing a suit improves your attitude. You behave better when you dress up."

Feeling exhausted and weakened from his pain, Netar sat on the courthouse steps. Without caring about how he looked or sounded, he began a prayer of anguish. Most people strolled by as if he was invisible while some strained to comprehend what sounded like incessant mumbling. His actions even caused a few people's heads to turn as they passed him, even though it was quite common to see people talking to themselves publically in downtown Atlanta.

Netar appeared like an oddity because rarely had anyone seen someone so good-looking and well-dressed babble to himself in such a manner. People got the impression that what he was doing wasn't a part of his normal, daily routine and they became curious about his behavior. Faintly aware that he was becoming a spectacle, Netar lowered his voice, but continued to pray. With his head down in despair, he didn't notice some of the onlookers struggling not to stare. He also didn't see the heavily-tattooed, young man carefully and menacingly watching him from a corner, as he secretly recorded his emotional diatribe.

Oblivious to the menagerie of strangers around him, Netar pleaded with God to anoint him as a spiritual mercenary. He reminded Him that throughout history He had used men to destroy His enemies. He recited the scripture about *a time to kill.* He petitioned God to protect him; and strengthen him to remove Kaseem, an evil menace from the world.

He queried, *"How could it be Your will, Heavenly Father, that this man should escape justice after raping and beating my sister to death? Aren't You omniscient? Haven't You seen all the innocent people this man has murdered, raped, terrorized, and poisoned with drugs? I know that you are a just God and would not have more blood flooding the streets. I am your servant; use me to do Your will."*

After his tormented moment of supplication, he closed his eyes, lifted his head, and let the sun kiss his handsome face. As he tried to mentally block out the noisy world swirling around him, a feeling of peace gradually started to permeate his mind, body, and spirit. He knew God had heard his prayers. He also knew that killing Kaseem would be an act of divine justice, not vengeance.

He wasn't overly concerned about the

details of how and when he would complete his mission. He just felt good knowing that God wasn't going to allow his sister's killer to hurt more people.

In due time was the answer that God had placed in his heart. Before Netar had a chance to get up and find his family, he heard his brother, Linford, calling him. When he turned around, he was pleased to see that his mother had stopped crying.

Netar walked toward his mother with opened arms and gave her a warm, lingering hug. Then he whispered in her ear that everything would be alright. She responded by doing something she hadn't done in almost two years — she managed a small, genuine smile.

Chapter 2
God

While God sits high, He looks low. God had indeed heard Netar. And, while He always answers prayers, His answer is not always, "yes". Sometimes it is a resounding, "no". Other times, it's later — maybe, if the person can handle the blessing.

Nevertheless, God felt that Netar was justified in his request. He had witnessed Kaseem's perpetual evil and while He didn't always interfere in humans' lives as they prescribed, He decided that He would oblige Netar.

God rejoiced that Netar was special. His good heart pleased Him. And, even though Netar had so many opportunities to turn away from Him, he strove to live a righteous life. Of course, God recognized that he wasn't perfect; Netar made mistakes as every other human being did, but the average young man with his intellect, body and wealth succumbed to destructive temptation at the drop of a dime. Yet, Netar had remained humble, focused on Him, and able to see beyond the traps satan had set for men.

Three Nights in December

Netar stood out because he genuinely cared about others. He was always demonstrating compassion, especially for "the least of these." When Netar was a teenager, he promised God that he would try to empower at least one person each day.

But now God saw that Netar's heart had become hardened after his sister's death. He was bitter about what seemed like a horrible injustice.

At the same time, Netar had begun blaming himself for the incident. While he appeared to maintain a normal life including managing his business, he was mentally tormented by thinking of a thousand things he could have done to prevent the tragedy. Moreover, he was struggling to control his rabid temper every time he thought of Kaseem.

It was only the prayers of others that had stopped him from killing Kaseem with his bare hands on the day of the trial. Now, he often fantasized about getting in his car, finding Kaseem and opening his jugular! Because of grace, he was able to keep telling himself that he had to be disciplined to destroy his enemy; the right time would come though. And, he would be ready.

C. Chérie Hardy

At some point, Netar started smoking marijuana occasionally. Under the constant radar of his family, he secretly grew his own special supply behind a shed in his backyard. Using the herb though made him feel like he was betraying God.

Up until the moment his sister died, he believed men should only get a natural high that emanated from the Holy Spirit. In fact, he used to criticize his friends who smoked *weed,* and often called them cowards for trying to avoid "the real world" and their true emotions.

"What a hypocrite I am!" Netar would often say to himself, as he smoked weed at night on his patio.

God, on the other hand, was keeping a tight surveillance on Netar. He knew that Netar hadn't lost his faith in Him. He admired Netar for being stronger than most men who thought He was less powerful and less worthy of praise because He didn't always rescue them from their trouble.

When people did this, it didn't hurt God's feelings, but it often astonished Him. He was blamed for everything, yet He didn't pull the trigger; rob the bank; purchase the alcohol and drugs; oppress the fatherless and the poor; rape children; and hate. Humans did! Every second of the day people were conjuring up new and interesting ways to destroy THEMSELVES. It was a vicious cycle that hurt God's heart.

It seemed no matter how many times He tried to articulate how much He loved people, they still rejected Him. It wasn't the other way around. Oh no! People were always slamming the door in God's face. But, if they had done that a thousand times, He would have forgiven them because contrary to popular belief, He is, and always has been, a loving, compassionate, generous and forgiving God.

However, God decided a long time ago that He was not going to operate like a gangster. He wasn't going to force humans to do His will. After all, He wouldn't be the Perfect Gentleman if He did. Mankind had created torture, not He. Somehow, humans had to understand that there are consequences built into every action they take.

And, God didn't change life, He changed people. He was like a Master Teacher showing them how get the rich lessons from all they experienced in life. He longed to show His children that in every trial, there is a treasure, but only the GOOD TEACHER can help people find priceless, spiritual jewels hidden beneath the pain. It's sad that so few ever bothered to show up for class.

God just wished that people could understand that He wasn't just sitting in Heaven checking a punishment scroll and destroying them for every little thing they did. In fact, while He often chastened those He loved like a good father would, He didn't want to destroy His people whom He considered priceless masterpieces. How much sense did that make? He wanted to save His people — all of them. But again, He refused to twist people's arm to get them to do things that would create life instead of death.

God decided the time had come for Him to introduce Netar to Adara. He smiled thinking how their minds and hearts would be healed through tragedy. In God's irrefutable wisdom, He decided that even though Netar would take one life, he would save two, including his own.

God had already chosen the special woman that Netar would love before he was conceived. Eons ago, He had breathed love into each heart. This love could never be erased; not even death could destroy it. After all, as a poet once wrote, "[He] works in a mysterious way and, His wonders to perform. He plants His footsteps in the sea and rides upon the storm."

The couple would seem like an incongruent pair at first. But, when Netar and Adara had surrendered to God's voice they would enjoy a love beyond their most beautiful dreams.

God rejoiced! He always had the perfect way of transforming tragedy into triumph. One day, Netar would accept that his beloved sister, Gitele, had not died in vain. He would eventually come to understand that God used his loss for a purpose — to lead him to an unconquerable love that would save his life.

C. Chérie Hardy

Chapter 3
Inventory

As an avid reader, Adara Jacobson had thoroughly enjoyed working as a library clerk at Hilliard University in Atlanta for the past three and a half years. On the other hand, completing the facility's inventory for the last few weeks had depleted her energy. This year the job was much more tedious and arduous than usual due to the university's budget cuts. While Hilliard boasted a student body of approximately five thousand students, the library's staff now consisted of only four people: two veteran librarians, Ms. Lurelia Cooper and Ms. Rosette Smith, as well as, two student-assistants, she and Ivisse Harris.

Sometimes this meant that everyone had to work for extended hours, often without pay. Adara didn't mind though and was grateful for the opportunity to work. She and Ivisse were both financially, disadvantaged seniors, and had remained grateful that they had been able to maintain their work-study jobs in spite of the university's recent financial woes.

Moreover, Adara would have done anything for Ms. Cooper who often reminded her of her beloved grandmother. The elderly and warmhearted sage had become a mentor to her and Ivisse. She appreciated that Ms. Cooper was fair and regularly went beyond the call of duty to support and encourage students to do their personal best. Moreover, the God-fearing woman inculcated spiritual wisdom whenever she could.

Adara also realized that without Ms. Cooper's insight, protection and guidance, she might not have survived urban, college life. Being extremely sheltered as a child, and growing up in a small town in North Carolina, Adara had had a difficult time adjusting to some of the cultural and social norms of a big city like Atlanta. She couldn't thank Ms. Cooper enough for helping her work through her transitional shock during her freshman year of college.

As the library staff got closer to completing its special task, fortunately the Christmas break started. Additionally, snow was coming, and there was nothing that could clear the streets faster in Atlanta than a few drops of the white stuff. With less student traffic and distractions in the library, the women would have more time for their work.

The bad news was that Ivisse was leaving

the crew earlier than expected.

Her parents had purchased a nonrefundable airline ticket several months ago. There was no way she could postpone her trip back home to California for a few more days to help complete the inventory. While everyone was glad that Ivisse would be spending time with her family, it was hard not to admit that she would be missed in more ways than one.

However, even though Adara was fatigued from her job, she kept a smile on her face. She was excited about just finishing the first half of her senior year. The disappointment she endured because she wouldn't be able to go home for the holidays due to some unexpected graduation fees, was lessened each time she remembered that she only had four more months of undergraduate school. Being able to return home prepared to serve and teach children in her community motivated her to stay focused and work hard.

When the inventory was finally done, Adara kept thinking how nice it was going to be to finally get some rest and catch up on her reading during the break. Her small apartment which was located a few blocks from Hillard's campus didn't have all the amenities of a plush home, but she appreciated the privacy and solitude.

She had heard from Ivisse that residing in the dormitories could be a nightmare. She was regularly trying to dodge the drama that some young women got a twisted joy from starting. This made Adara grateful that her church had paid for her living expenses, so she didn't have the trouble that came with living among strangers.

To her surprise, Ms. Cooper gave her a beautifully wrapped box on the day she left for the break. She demanded that Adara not open it until Christmas. While Adara hadn't had the money to buy something for her mentor, she presented a special card to her in which she expressed heartfelt gratitude for all of the love and support Ms. Cooper had demonstrated over the years. She just wanted the faithful woman to know that she hadn't taken her for granted, and all of her kind deeds and words would always be cherished and remembered.

With Ivisse already departed, the three co-workers embraced, wished each other well, and the older ladies headed home. When Ms. Cooper inquired about Adara's transportation plans, she assured her that she had everything worked out. She knew if she told Ms. Cooper she was going to walk home at night, she would have insisted that she stay with her until morning. Adara, however, just couldn't convince herself to impose on a woman who had already done so much for her. But as she left the building and the cold air whipped across her face, she regretted she hadn't accepted Ms. Cooper's offer.

While she had been dreaming about reading a good book and soaking in a warm tub, she had forgotten about her dilemma of getting home safely in the snow. Finally, she convinced herself that she could endure a 25-minute walk. After bundling up, she headed toward her apartment in the dark, snowy night.

Chapter 4
The Alley

As soon as Adara exited the doors of the library, she wished she had made other arrangements for getting home. Glancing at her watch, she realized it was almost one o'clock in the morning, and in addition to being dark and cold, it was snowing. While the lighting was good in most areas of the campus, the streets were completely deserted. Furthermore, she'd have to walk through a secluded alley, alone. She shivered just from the thought.

Usually, even this late, the streets would be bustling with activity, but most students had already gone home for Christmas. About an inch of snow had accumulated on the roads, and with the steady stream that pelted Adara's face now, there would probably be at least two or three inches blanching cars and buildings by morning.

She took a deep breath and started hesitantly descending the stairs. There was simply no other way to get home, she thought. The buses didn't operate during the holidays, she didn't have money for a cab and she couldn't think of a single person she felt comfortable calling and asking to pick her up in the wee hours of the morning on such a wintry night.

Suddenly, Adara felt a surge of anxiety, but continued walking while adjusting her backpack on her shoulder and tightening her scarf around her neck. She still couldn't convince herself to call Ms. Cooper and ask if she could sleep on her sofa until morning. And, she knew Mrs. Smith would have refused anyway.

Adara imagined that her co-workers were warm, cozy, and already tucked into bed since they lived only five minutes from the library in a special dormitory for older faculty and staff members. She told herself she'd be home soon, too so that fear wouldn't paralyze her heart.

As she increased her pace, she remembered a phrase her grandmother used to say, "Sometimes you have to push aside your fear and show God how much you trust Him." For some reason she wasn't comforted by the saying as she had been many times in the past. Adara believed that there was a fine line between faith and foolishness, and wisdom was the key to discerning the difference. Even though she told herself to be strong, she fretted about whether or not she was making a wise choice at the moment.

Three Nights in December

Adara began reciting the twenty-third chapter of Psalm when she caught the first glimpse of the two buildings that created an alley which would remove her from the open view of the main, campus thoroughfares. The façade of each massive structure, one a lecture hall, and the other, a textbook warehouse, were in opposite directions. While students often took the road behind the buildings as a shortcut to save time during the day, it was rumored that awful things had happened over the years in the alley at night.

Other than student, foot-traffic during the regular school year, there was a large dumpster as well as a loading dock in the rear of each building. Over the years, students had been warned that the alley was potentially a criminal's idyllic location so most traveled in pairs or small groups at night, yet tonight Adara was alone — or so she thought.

C. Chérie Hardy

Chapter 5
Nightmare

When Netar discovered that Kaseem was stalking a young woman at Hilliard University, he decided to take matters into his own hands. The justice system had already failed his family and too many others. Kaseem's character was no big secret around town. The only mystery that no one could solve was how a man, notorious for heinous crimes against innocent and defenseless women and children, could continue to roam the streets unchecked.

But, tonight would be the last time Kaseem would ever *attempt* to hurt another human being. For the past year, Netar had been keeping a watchful eye on Kaseem's movements. At some point, it became clear to him that Kaseem's next target was a beautiful college student who appeared oblivious that she had become prey to one of the devil's favorite sons.

A few times Netar had seen Kaseem offering her a ride and even trying to start a conversation with her while she waited at a bus stop in front of the library. Thank God though the young woman had ignored and rejected Kaseem's advances even though her actions only fueled his sick mind.

As Kaseem moved into the alley to act out his vile fantasies on a helpless lamb, Netar was one step ahead of him. He had already parked his truck in the loading dock at the farthest end of the alley, stashed the materials he needed dispose of Kaseem's body and placed his unregistered and untraceable, loaded gun with a silencer in his jacket pocket. He knew that Kaseem's car was also already in the other dock, tucked away from public view.

After the girl took a few steps in the alley, Kaseem started his pursuit. He had been charting her movements for the entire day and couldn't believe how easy she had made it for him by walking in the alley alone. He almost burst out with laughter when he saw her frightened eyes as she walked into his snare. He had planned to abduct her from the alley, take her to his *special* apartment and rape her for as long as her body would last. She wouldn't think rejection was so easy again he thought to himself. He imagined with utter delight that when he'd finished releasing his terror, he would kill her and dump her body in a place where she'd never be found. *Never be found*. That thought delighted Kaseem very much.

C. Chérie Hardy

After his last trial, he vowed to do a better job of covering up his dirt. A few of the judges, lawyers and police officers on his payroll had decided to voluntarily sever ties with him after to his infamous "not guilty" verdict which caused so much outrage in the city. When a deluge of organizations from all over the country descended upon Atlanta to protest what they saw was a blatant injustice, people decided to distance themselves from him. A few politicians had even lost their re-election bids because of the incident. That's when Kaseem vowed he would never get caught again.

When Adara heard something behind her that sounded like a man coughing, she turned her head. Immediately she felt her heart sank to her feet when she saw a man completely dressed in black following her. His face seemed vaguely familiar although she couldn't remember when or where she'd met him. His eyes danced wildly and were filled with basilisk lust. Adara instinctively knew the man intended to harm her and she started to run.

Her brain told her to scream, but when she opened her mouth, sound evaporated into the cold air. Her backpack was weighing her down, so she dropped it to the ground. Just as she heard its loud thud on the snow-covered asphalt, another man appeared before her. He popped up from behind the dumpster like a tall, dark ghost. She shrieked and tried to step back.

But with the celerity of a master fighter of jiu jitsu, Netar firmly grabbed Adara who was only a few feet from Kaseem's hateful grip. Pivoting with the speed of lightning, he shoved her away as gently as he could before he aimed and fired his gun right between Kaseem's eyes. The beast never knew what hit him and crumbled to the ground like a cheap ragdoll. The silencer on his gun made sure no one heard the shot. For good measure, Netar shot him three more times, twice in his chest and another between his eyes.

From Netar's peripheral he saw the girl moving. He had unintentionally pushed her down and she was now trying to get up. He reached her with a few large steps and easily wrapped her tightly in his arms. "I won't hurt you. Don't move," he whispered in her ear.

Adara stiffened as tears involuntarily started to flow from her eyes. She felt so lightheaded she feared she would faint.

"Please," she whimpered softly as she felt her body becoming weaker each second.

But Netar tightened his grip. "You must trust me. I will not hurt you. Don't move and listen," he continued.

"Take out your cell phone," Netar said firmly. He had to make sure that the frightened, young woman couldn't call the police.

"I...I... It's in my backpack. I dropped it as I was running," Adara responded nervously.

"Okay, I will get it. Now pay attention. You are going to have to sit in my truck for about twenty minutes. I promise to let you go, but there are some things we must discuss first. If I was going to hurt you, I would not have saved your life. I just need to take care of some things to ensure your safety. When I lock the truck, don't be alarmed. You won't be able to open the doors anyway."

Hearing those words, Adara attempted futilely to get out of Netar's grasp. However, her small, weakened body was no match for his six feet four, 230-pound, muscled physique. "I promise I will not harm you," he reiterated as he quickly opened the door of the truck and gently placed Adara on the back seat.

Netar locked his truck and vanished as fast as he had appeared. Even though the streets seemed deserted he knew he couldn't delay cleaning up the area and getting rid of Kaseem's car. In less than five minutes, he demagnetized Kaseem's phone and electronics and made them untraceable. Then he quickly rolled his body in a large tarpaulin. Afterwards he placed everything in a large trash bag which he reinforced by re-wrapping it several times. Next, he placed the remains in the dumpster. He was careful to move items around so that Kaseem's body bag was at the very bottom of the receptacle.

Thoroughly inspecting the ground, he quickly moved to Kaseem's car. He tossed his wallet, gun and several other items in a bag. Fortunately, several weeks earlier he had found out about a chop shop only seven minutes away from the campus. It was cleverly hidden behind an abandoned building that was surrounded by large pine trees. It would be hard, even for law enforcement to spot. He had planned to take the car there and run back to his truck. He just hoped that the young woman wasn't trying to escape or harm herself.

When Netar got to the chop shop he was greeted by two heavily, armed men. While he looked intimidating, especially with his hooded face and black clothing, he was no match to their weaponry. Although he wasn't necessarily trying to hide his identity, the winter clothing obscured his face and body. The men studied Netar carefully. In their line of work, they had to be ready for an ambush every second of the day and night.

"Greetings," Netar said, his deep voice vibrated through the cold, night air. However, the men remained silent while keeping their baleful eyes on the mysterious, uninvited stranger and their fingers on the trigger.

"Gentlemen, this car is a special gift," Netar said as he tossed the keys to one of the men. While the guys looked at each other perplexed, he continued, "The parts are worth thousands and it is loaded with goodies. Merry Christmas, my friends," he said while cautiously watching the men.

Netar made sure he didn't move until he knew the men had clearly interpreted his words. He kept his eyes alert and maintained an expressionless face. When the men smiled and their bright, gold teeth glowed in the darkness, he knew he had earned their trust.

Each man nodded as a way of communicating his appreciation and reached out to firmly shake Netar's gloved hand. Netar was relieved that things had gone as predicted. The men recognized a good deal when they found one. In fact, they admired this stranger and wished he had time to talk awhile. In the history of their felonious security duty, they hadn't ever had someone *bring* a car to them.

"Good night," my brothers, Netar said lightly.

"Anytime my nigga," one of men responded.

"Come back, nigga, if yo' ass get mo' cars," the other man offered before Netar vanished in the night like a phantom.

Meanwhile Adara sat restless in Netar's truck trying to process what had just happened. She couldn't believe that she had survived an assault; yet had been rescued; and had witnessed a murder, all in a matter of two minutes. She must be dreaming. She told herself that at any moment, she would awake and discover that everything that had transpired in the last hour wasn't real.

A thousand thoughts sprinted through Adara's mind at once. She contemplated blowing the horn of the truck to get attention. She thought of breaking a window, but how? What if she couldn't escape? She wondered what

C. Chérie Hardy

the giant stranger meant when he said, *"There are some things we must discuss first."* What things? She was so exhausted and frightened she didn't even have the strength to fight. She was trying to calm down and think, but she felt so lightheaded.

As each new and troubling thought began to swim around her mind, her body trembled uncontrollably. In an effort to slow down her rapidly beating, spastic heart, she began to pray. "Heavenly Father, please help me. Jesus, please save me," she said aloud. Her answer appeared at the door of his truck holding her backpack. The mysterious, darkly-clothed man had returned.

Chapter 6
Late Night Rendezvous

Netar didn't like what he was doing, but in all his planning to kill Kaseem, he hadn't spent time thinking about the girl and how her role might affect his actions. Here she was sitting in his truck terrified and obviously tired and he hadn't decided what he should do. As methodical and meticulous as he was, he'd forgotten to prepare for this mockingbird that was now a witness to his crime.

For several moments they drove in silence, each following the rhythm of the other's heartbeat. Netar broke the monotony by trying to apologize and explain himself.

"I know you are afraid right now and I hate you've had to endure what happened tonight. I want you to know that I will release you, but there are some things I have to work out first and I need some time to think. Do you understand me?"

He paused and reflected on his next words. "Don't be alarmed, but you will have to stay with me for the next few days."

At that moment, Adara couldn't hold back her silent tears. Her terror was palpable in

29

the small space of the truck and she began to weep softly and shake her head in disbelief.

"I am sorry. You must trust me. I promise to release you physically unharmed. I don't want to disturb you, but you need to know that the man I killed earlier savagely beat my younger sister to death a few years ago. Somehow, he managed to get off because of some legal loophole or technicality. It might be wrong, but I vowed to make sure he wouldn't hurt anyone else. And, that's exactly what he was going to do to you tonight."

Again, Netar paused allowing his words to penetrate the young woman. "I don't regret what I did. I had to protect you, but I have to make sure that no one ever knows about what happened. Can you promise that you will keep this a secret?"

Adara was silent for several seconds before managing to say, "Yes". She hoped this meant the man would immediately release her. "I promise not to tell a soul. I am grateful that you saved my life, but please let me go," she said softly.

"I will," Netar responded as he continued to drive to his next destination. The snow was steadily falling, and he knew by morning the streets might not be drivable if they turned icy. He decided to stop by Walmart to get food and allow the young woman to get some personal items and toiletries. He would explain more to her when they got to his home.

Adara sat quietly in Netar's truck as she watched the snow slowly descend from the nebulous sky. She had no idea where she was going since she hadn't ever ventured too far from Hilliard's campus. Furthermore, she had never learned to drive. While in Atlanta she had only used the public transit system to travel. At some point it dawned on her that she hadn't paid attention to the road signs and couldn't figure out what interstate they were on.

She tried taking extended, deep breaths to relax her heart which had picked up speed again. She desperately wanted to believe the stranger who had just saved her life, but she became more nervous as they sped farther down the highway. She suddenly remembered what an instructor had said during freshman orientation: "Never let an abductor take you to a second location. Your chances of survival are significantly decreased."

Netar interrupted Adara's thoughts by introducing himself. He decided that it would be

31

okay if she knew his name. "I hate we didn't have proper introductions, but my name is Netar Moore," he said with a sharply masculine voice spiced with a strong New York accent.

"What is your name? And, where are you from?" he asked.

"My name is Adara Jacobson and I'm from a small town in North Carolina called Matam," Adara said in a barely audible volume.

"I am pleased to meet you, Adara. I hate it was under these circumstances though." Then he added, hoping some light chatter would help the girl relax, "I didn't know there was a city called Matam in the United States. There is one in Senegal. I learned about it years ago while in high school."

"Matam is so small that it's not even on a map. It was founded by liberated African slaves before the Civil War. Its history is so unique and obscure, most people have never heard of it. It's one of America's best kept secrets."

"It sounds interesting. I hope I can learn more, later," Netar said. Then he continued, "I know you're not going to like what I am about to say, but we are going to stop by Walmart. I want you to pick up enough clothing for the next three days. With this inclement weather, we might be locked in for some time. Make sure you get all the personal items you need. We are also going to get something to eat. The last time there was a snow storm in Atlanta, the grocery store in my neighborhood ran out of food. Trucks couldn't get into the city because of ice on the roads. We don't want to be in that situation."

As Netar entered Walmart's parking lot, he examined Adara's face from his rearview mirror. He was trying to gage her emotions. He didn't want things to go from bad to worse. He could see the girl was still afraid and anxious. She might try to make a run for it in the store.

He parked the truck and then said as gently as he could, "I don't like saying this, but if you try to escape, I will shoot you. You will fall to the ground and no one will know what happened and where the bullet came from. I really hate threatening you, Adara, but I can't jeopardize my family's safety. I promise that if you comply, we won't have any problems. I'll walk behind you in the store. I know it's hard but try not to look too frightened. You'll only draw more attention to yourself. Do you understand me?"

Adara was dumbstruck for a few moments. The idea that this man would shoot her without a second thought made her tremble. She had already seen what Netar was capable of doing and knew that he wasn't making idle threats. Imagining her grandmother being called and told that her lifeless body was found on the store's floor caused a new surge of emotions to attack her heart, but she managed to respond affirmatively to his question.

"Yes. I understand you," she replied, her voice quivering with each syllable.

Trying to calm the girl's fragile state of mind, Netar said, "Look, I don't want to hurt you. I pray that this nightmare will be over soon. And, I promise that when I return you to your home, you will never see me again. I just need to sort through some things first. Trust me I deeply regret what's happening. I really do."

Adara finally exhaled the breath she had been holding. She had avoided eye contact with Netar throughout the entire night, but she lifted her head and allowed herself to look into his dark eyes for a few seconds. She was trying to read his thoughts. One minute he sounded like a gentleman; another, he sounded like a brute.

He was verbally articulate, and she suspected well-educated. On the other hand, his threats, which she had no doubts he would act upon, were disturbing. Furthermore, the expression on his ebony-toned face was indiscernible. In fact, she regretted that she had tried to gaze into his eyes which seemed to sear through her body like exploding, hot coals.

Netar was a master at concealing his feelings. He knew Adara was deciding whether or not to attempt an escape. He allowed a few moments of silence to pass between them. He let his thoughts saunter around the small space of the truck. Knowing that she had gotten the right message, he said, "Are you ready?"

"I...I... I don't have... have... any money to get things," Adara stammered.

"That's not a problem," Netar answered. "Get want you need, but let's not waste any more time."

For over an hour, Netar carefully studied his captive as they slowly navigated through the large store together. He couldn't help noticing the young woman's expression of pure terror, in spite of her sincere efforts to mask it. Thankfully, people seemed so preoccupied with getting supplies for the snow storm that they overlooked the young woman's pleading eyes. Netar was glad that he didn't have to use his gun for a second time.

Chapter 7
Adara

Netar was relieved that things had gone well in the store. When he insisted that Adara pick up some of the special food items, he was amazed that she only chose teas, lemons and organic sugar. As he drove to his home, she was so quiet that he had almost forgotten that she was with him.

It was hard for him to ignore how pretty she was as his eyes freely roamed over her face and body through his rearview mirror. Yet, she seemed oblivious of how her smooth, peanut-butter-colored skin; long, jet black, natural-textured hair; and eyes, a unique mélange of brown and orange, could affect men. Indeed, she was completely unaware of how her soft, pink, full lips could potentially drive a man insane.

If the exotic butterfly he was now transporting in his truck knew how appealing she was, she certainly didn't act like it. Her demureness seemed totally genuine. Her naïveté couldn't be feigned even if she had put forth her best effort to conceal it.

Netar had found himself more intrigued each time he watched her as Kaseem had. He was not surprised that his foe had added her to his menagerie of beautiful victims, but the girl was an enigma.

She always wore oversized clothing and didn't seem to date at all. He noticed whenever a male would try to converse with her at the bus stop, she would ignore him or walk away. The only times he'd seen her smile, talk or laugh was when she was interacting with the older women and/or her classmate from the library.

In a world where women flaunted their bodies shamelessly, Netar wondered if she was hiding something. His curiosity about what was underneath all those layers of heavy fabric was starting to consume him. Maybe there was something hideous she didn't want anyone to see.

While he knew quite a few modest women, he had never met a female who had made so much effort to purposely conceal her figure. Being conservative was not a crime or sin, but she had taken things to a level he had never known.

Netar imagined that if he had passed Adara on the street as a stranger, he wouldn't have noticed her. And, that's exactly what he detected she was trying to do — become invisible to men. When he looked at her again in his rearview mirror, she had finally fallen asleep.

Her face looked so angelic and peaceful. Based on the behavior he had observed before tonight, he suspected that she had been sheltered. Her naïveté and innocence were almost tangible. He pondered about the intimate details of her youth in a small town — one that's not even on a map, must have been compared to his own in New York city. Their lives must have been completely opposite. And, Netar resolved it was best to keep his distance, but not until he had gotten at least one peek of what was underneath all those layers of clothing, he told himself.

Later, Netar scolded himself for getting distracted. As a man, he knew he was starting to feel pure, unadulterated lust for Adara. She had captured his attention, but he reminded himself that he had to be disciplined in order to avoid more problems. He called the girl's name before hesitantly touching her shoulder to awaken her. She opened her eyes quickly, not registering where she was for a few seconds.

"We're at my house, now," Netar's voice jolted her memory. "I'll show you the guest room and get your things, so you can get some sleep. The roads are icy as predicted, so I might not be able to get you home until Monday morning. Follow me."

In her sleepy haze of consciousness, Adara was awed by the size and the luxurious furnishings of the house. She quietly followed Netar, yet not feeling any less nervous than before. She warily watched Netar as he opened the door to a bedroom with a bed so big that she blinked several times. She didn't know a bed that size existed. The thought that she was in a man's house she didn't even know unsettled her. She had never been alone with a man in her 21-year-old life.

"The linen is clean, but there's a closet next to the bathroom if you need anything," Netar said.

Netar turned on the light in the bathroom. "There are towels, soap and whatever you need in there. I'll unload your stuff in a few minutes. Do you want anything to eat or drink?"

"Could I have some water, please?" Adara asked.

"Sure." Netar pointed to the small refrigerator on a table in the bedroom. "In the morning you can cook whatever you want to eat."

"Thank you," Adara responded with a small voice.

"Try to get some rest," Netar added as he left to get the bags from the car.

Adara just sat nervously on the bed as Netar brought in her things. For some reason, she almost cried when he laid her backpack in front of her. But, as soon as he put it down, her cell phone rang. The sound startled her, and she literally jumped.

Netar and Adara eyes met for a brief moment. "You're expecting a call from your boyfriend?" Netar quipped.

"No. No...I don't have one. It's my grandmother. I know she's worried sick about me. I always call her before I go to bed each night. Please let me answer her call. She's old and alone. Please. I... I will convince her that I am alright. Please. I promise not to say anything about you."

Netar searched Adara's eyes until she looked away. "Okay," he reluctantly agreed. The phone had stopped ringing as he leaned upon the door frame to watch Adara. His eyes felt like fire bombs all over body, so she tried to turn her head. "Face me and put the speaker on," he said in a tone harsher than he intended. He didn't believe a word she said about "a grandmother."

While keeping her eyes on Netar, Adara picked up her phone and slowly called her grandmother. When the old woman answered the phone, her voice sounded very tired and worried.

"Hi Grandma," Adara said while trying to stop her voice from trembling.

"Adara. Jesus! I have been so worried about you. Are you okay? I have been trying to call you all night."

"Yes ma'am. I am so sorry I didn't call you, but I just got in. It's snowing here in Atlanta and I was stuck on the bus for a few hours, but I am fine now. I am getting ready to take a bath and go to bed." She tried to turn her head away from Netar again, but he cleared his throat and she knew exactly what that meant.

"Thank the Lord, sugar. I knew He would take care of my grandchild," Adara's grandmother said as she let out a loud sigh of relief. "Well, I know you don't have many minutes on your phone, so I will let you go, but I wanted to check on you and say, 'I love you'. Lord, I feel so much better hearing your voice. I wish you could be here for Christmas, but I know those fees took every penny you had.

Well…, good night. I will talk to you again soon."

"I will look forward to that. I love you, too, Grandma," Adara said before hanging up the phone while keeping her eyes on Netar.

"Can I trust you with that phone?" he asked while coming closer to her.

Trying to ignore his height and size, she said, "Yes. If it makes you feel better, take it. All I ask is that you please let me answer the phone if my grandmother calls. I promise not to say anything about what happened," she pleaded.

After studying Adara's face for a few moments, Netar said, "Okay, I'll let you keep it. Try to get some sleep," he whispered before leaving and closing the door of the bedroom.

Adara sat frozen for a few minutes while staring at the closed door. Eventually, she came out of her trance and began quietly praying for God's protection and mercy as she unpacked her things. After taking a much needed shower, she lay in bed and she let a montage of the night's events replay in her mind. The strange things she had experienced were surreal and she clung to the idea that she still might wake up and discover she had been dreaming.

Struggling to keep her eyes open, she

wondered if she should call the police or her grandmother. This seemed like the perfect time to attempt an escape. However, she believed that God was telling her to be still because Netar wouldn't hurt her despite his threats and intimidating looks.

As exhausted as she was, she said one final prayer for Netar. As soon as she closed her eyes, she went into a deep, peaceful sleep.

Chapter 8
Netar

It was four o'clock in the morning when Netar finally reclined on the large sectional in his living room. He had managed to check on Adara undetected after taking his shower. Seeing her sleeping peacefully in bed moved him. Like a moth to a light, he found himself emotionally drawn to her. Unexpectedly, she became more engrossing to him with each passing minute they shared together. He also felt an overwhelming need to protect her. Thinking about how Kaseem would have hurt her made his blood pressure instantly rise.

As a desirable and educated 25-year- old with money, good looks and charm, he had never had a problem attracting women. Being a star football player in college could have made him a playboy. However, he had been taught by the strong, honorable Black men in his family to value a woman's mind and heart. He was also keenly aware of the consequences of uncommitted relationships and casual sex.

Over the years, he'd met older men from all walks of life. He could only think of a few who didn't have some horror story to tell about women. He knew men who had contracted diseases; had their tires slashed; or found out they were raising another man's child. Their lives became warnings about unwanted pregnancies, financial woes, life-threatening drama and so many more headaches. These men often felt frustrated and found it hard to celebrate women. They were always reminding Netar to be careful and stay away from unscrupulous women.

At the same time, most of those same men never gave up on finding a good woman. The only problem they'd say is meeting one would be like finding an eighty-carat diamond in your backyard. Additionally, because of their own distrust of women and negative experiences, they ended up sabotaging relationships.

To his credit, Netar decided to heed the wisdom of his elders. He learned to avoid that kind of trouble by being very selective about the women with whom he became closely involved.

While he dated often and had even indulged in a couple of long-term, sexual liaisons, he had not met anyone with whom he wanted to start a committed relationship. This disappointed a few women who had mistakenly believed that their beauty and/or bedroom

45

antics would get them down the aisle.

It was just that after conversing with many women, he had failed to find someone like his mother who possessed a quiet strength and who valued home life more than she did collecting shoes or handbags. And while being formally educated, articulate and focused on serving others would be traits he'd want in his ideal woman, he was willing to work with someone who was open to growing and learning how to be a better human being. Unfortunately, it seemed that he was asking for too much since most of the women he'd known were selfish, haughty, and only concerned about getting what *they* wanted.

At the same time, he knew good women were everywhere. His mother, aunts, sister-in-law and even his late sister were all examples of righteous women. But his quandary had been finding someone who didn't see him as an ATM machine, a potential "baby-daddy", or a sex god. His older brother, Linford, would often tease him about his prolonged bachelorhood.

Linford, who was happily married with three sons, had met his wife, Charlotte when he was twenty-two years old. He often liked to say it was love at first sight although his wife has a

different recollection of their meeting.
Nevertheless, he would often describe how
Charlotte had captured his attention. She was a
volunteer for a special literacy program at one of
the local schools in one of the roughest areas of
New York.

Linford and Charlotte met when one of
his college professors required that all of his
seniors complete a certain number of community
service hours. Linford often said that he knew
that Charlotte was "the one" after seeing her
read to a child with so much passion. Later he
found out that although she came from a
wealthy family, she was not materialistic. She
also appreciated Linford for who he was and not
for what he could buy her.

Linford would often say, "A man could
be the most decent human being in the world,
bro, but if a woman doesn't value his goodness,
the relationship will be miserable and won't
last."

"That appreciation only comes when a
woman has a personal relationship with God.
She has to see you as a blessing in order show
how grateful she is for all the things you do.
That's why I married Charlotte. And, one day
God will bless you with a good woman, too," he
added.

C. Chérie Hardy

As Netar reflected about Adara, he wondered if he had finally found his own personal *oasis* in the harsh, arid world that surrounded him. There was something that he couldn't understand or describe that made him intensely attracted to her. All he knew was that he hadn't been able to shake it off since the first moment he saw her several months ago when he started tracking Kaseem.

Now that he had finally met Adara, he realized there was something about her presence that changed the ambience of their shared space — it was peaceful and soothing. He couldn't remember ever experiencing that with another woman. It didn't make sense to him, but the feeling lingered and he couldn't shake it off no matter how hard he tried.

During the months he had watched Adara he found himself desiring to hear her voice, share his most intimate thoughts with her, and go places with her. He had also allowed himself to imagine himself making passionately love to her. It all felt so strange because he didn't even know her. All he knew was that his determination to kill Kaseem became heightened after he learned that she had become his next victim.

Three Nights in December

Sometimes he'd chide himself for getting caught up with what he thought was infatuation. He was convinced that the novel feelings he was having for Adara would eventually fade away. However, the more time he spent connected to her life, whether close-up and personal or from a distance, the more convinced he became that she might be "the one". That idea made Netar have the sweetest dreams.

Chapter 9
Plans

Netar and Adara both awoke in the afternoon around the same time. When she opened the door of the bedroom, Netar couldn't help noticing how refreshed she looked. It pleased him greatly to see that she seemed a bit more relaxed. Of course, she was wearing her usual oversized clothing that consisted of black sweat pants and a blue tee-shirt. She greeted him with a quizzical look and with a timorous tone asked if she could use his kitchen.

"Sure. Follow me," he replied as he led her into the kitchen. "Did you get any sleep?"

"Yes, I did. Thank you. What can I cook? Is there anything you want to eat?" she asked slowly.

"Well, you're a southern girl, aren't you?"

"Yes, I was born and raised in North Carolina," Adara responded plainly.

"So, I am going to trust that you can make salmon croquettes and grits."

"If you've got the ingredients, I can handle it," Adara said embarrassed that her stomach was growling loudly as she spoke.

"Okay. Help yourself to anything in the

kitchen. Later, we need to discuss a few things. I just checked the weather report. Not surprisingly, the snow and ice are causing a lot of problems on the roads. We might be stuck for maybe two more days, but I promise to get you back to Hilliard safely. Anyway, I need to take care of some business. Let me know when the food is ready. I'll be in the living room."

Adara nodded and immediately started preparing their meal. She hadn't eaten anything since yesterday morning and her stomach had literally started to cry out. While she quietly worked in the kitchen, she eavesdropped on Netar's conversations. Based on what she heard, she inferred that he owned some kind of business. It seemed that the weather had increased their revenue. Also, he was planning to travel to New York for Christmas.

When the food was ready, she handed him a note instead of interrupting his conversation. Even though he ended his call abruptly, it was clear that he had more things to discuss.

"It smells good in here," he said as he entered the kitchen. "I can't wait to taste what my southern gourmet has prepared," he teased.

"Well, now that you've become a food critique, please post an article in the AJC about me because it's going to be good." she volleyed back.

All Netar could do is smile and shake his head. What a difference a good night's sleep had made, he thought to himself. While they enjoyed some light jesting, he knew that there were some serious matters they needed to talk about.

"Could we pray together?" Netar said, completely surprising Adara. The expression on her face communicated, *"You pray?"*

"I know it could be hard to accept that I believe in God after last night, but I do. Adara, please know that I've asked God to forgive me for what I've put to you through, and I promised Him that I would make it up to you."

Netar seems sincere Adara thought to herself, but she just didn't know what to believe after what she'd witnessed in the alley. Nevertheless, she agreed to the prayer while trying not to be consumed with fear, which was constantly trying to resurface.

After saying a prayer, and taking a few bites of food, he started the conversation that could no longer be put off. "Adara, I want to apologize to you again for what you had to endure. As I shared with you earlier, the man I killed raped and beat Gitele, my baby sister to death. I know it might have looked like vengeance, but stopping evil sometimes is an act of justice that God ordains. Just as Kaseem killed my sister, he would have killed you. I don't regret protecting you, but there are some things we need to discuss since you were a witness to my crime."

"First, you must pledge that you will never tell a soul about what happened. At some point people are going to realize that Kaseem is missing. While I doubt his disappearance will cause the police to do an investigation, we can't be certain. I found out through the grapevine some months ago that Kaseem had a long list of enemies who were waiting for a chance to wipe him out. After the trial and the outrage over the verdict, a lot of attention was given to domestic violence and crime in general in the city. The Atlanta Police Department increased their presence in some of the most violent and drug-infested neighborhoods."

"As you can imagine the honest and law-abiding citizens appreciated this. On the other hand, the city's hoodlums were upset and blamed Kaseem for all the business they lost.

C. Chérie Hardy

Many of them had to either stop or move their drug and prostitution operations for several months until things cooled down. One of the biggest gang chiefs in Atlanta is rumored to have put a bounty on Kaseem's head," Netar continued.

"There was also word on the street that the police had planned to kill Kaseem. Some of them quickly severed ties with him and got off his payroll after the trial, but he still owed them money for past favors. Furthermore, they were tired of trying to cover up his dirt. Some corrupt cops believed that Kaseem would eventually expose how dishonorable they were; killing Kaseem would prevent this from ever happening."

"Kaseem has other enemies. One of them is an elderly man in his neighborhood. I understand that this guy was pretty heated with him after he biffed his wife in the face. So you can see no one will probably be trying to find out what happened to the menace. In fact, people will probably be happy to learn he's no longer around," Netar said.

"Finally, there is one last thing I need to add. It's one of the most shocking things I've heard. Kaseem had a sister, Yazmine who attended Hilliard when my sister was killed. She and Gitele had become friends at some point. In fact, it was Yazmine who had introduced the two of them."

"At first, things were going well. Yazmine, Kaseem and Gitele would hang out. When Gitele started getting behind in her classes, she decided to stop going out with Kaseem so she could improve her grades and get focused again. He took it personal and well…you know the rest of the disgusting story."

"When Kaseem's sister found out that he was accused of killing her dear friend, she started to lose her mind. Most people believe that Yazmine was not aware or ever involved in her family's crime life, but she still harbored quite a bit of guilt and shame after Gitele died. She blamed herself for the tragedy. To make matters worse, she was alienated from her relatives when she announced that she would testify against her brother. She knew that she was biting the hand that fed her, but she was willing to do anything to get justice for my sister," Netar continued.

"Yazmine also suffered because of her biological connection with Kaseem. Thinking she was as guilty as he was, some people began to harass and bully her around Hilliard's campus. She had become popular for all the wrong reasons and there was no place she could escape without someone implicating her in my sister's death. Many people insisted that she was involved even though all the evidence proves she was completely innocent."

"After the trial, people said that Yazmine just lost hope and started acting strangely. She started talking to herself publically, not grooming herself and eventually dropped out of school. Unfortunately, one day she was hit by a semi-truck while crossing the street. Some say it was suicide; others believe that due to her mental state she accidently walked into traffic. But the darkest and most unforgiving rumor is that Kaseem had his own sister killed for testifying against him." Netar ended.

"Incredible," Adara said. "This is the saddest story I've ever heard in my life. It's hard to believe people can be so savage. Those two young women didn't have to die so senselessly. And, it makes me sick to think how close I was to being killed by him, too."

"With all you've shared and Kaseem's character being so evil, do you think people would care about what had happened to a man who cold-bloodedly killed two young women? It's doubtful that his disappearance would ruffle any feathers, but with the world being so crazy these days, I guess anything can happen," Adara said thoughtfully.

"Don't worry angel, if we stick together, there will be no drama for both of us. Here's what I've been thinking: If the police question me I will tell them the truth, but of course, leave out the crime."

Adara looked at him puzzled.

"If I am questioned, I must have an alibi. I've decided to say that I saw you stranded in the snow and offered to help you. We got stuck in traffic. The road to your apartment was impassable so I offered you a warm place to stay. We went to Walmart. You stayed here until I could take you back home. When the snow eventually melted, we carried on our normal lives."

"But what if they ask why you were in the area? If we didn't know each other, why were you on Hilliard's campus?" Adara demanded.

"Good questions. You're smart. I'd say that I was checking on a job that my business was doing on campus. I own a heating and air company and we have had contracts with Hilliard for a few years. We do follow-up service checks periodically. No one from the college has to call us. It's one of the benefits of our service plan."

Netar carefully studied Adara's face. He knew she was totally committed to his plan. "Remember, the police probably won't look for Kaseem, but if they do, I've got every piece of the puzzle fitting perfectly into the alibi."

"The only two people who might look for Kaseem are his two brothers, Samuel and Jason." Netar took a deep breath and slowly shook his head. "Adara, I don't want you to get alarmed and trust me, I will protect you for the rest of your life, but we have to consider that they might start asking questions to find out if they could pin anyone to Kaseem's disappearance."

"I've heard that Kaseem's older brother has about six kids. People say he's gotten sentimental and he's trying to get out of criminal life and be a good father. At the same time, the street committee knows that Samuel was the brawn while Kaseem was the brain of their thug empire. Revenge killing is his specialty and he might feel obligated to avenge his brother. There's a blood-code that's not easily forgotten among thugs, especially for brothers who are partners in crime," Netar said.

"But the good news is that even though Samuel might try to do some investigating, he won't randomly kill anybody. From the long list of potential suspects who wanted Kaseem dead, he'll choose the person with the most circumstantial evidence pointed his way, and that wouldn't be me. And, with those six kids and three baby-mommas keeping his attention, he'll probably let things go."

"That leaves us with our only real threat, a dark horse that I still don't know too much about. He's Jason, Kaseem's younger brother. The word on the streets is that he's a coldhearted killer just like Kaseem. He's only sixteen and has already dropped out of school trying to create some street credit in the neighborhood. I am not worried about him at all because he's not methodical and disciplined like Kaseem. Hot heads usually die young in the hood."

Netar could see that Adara was trying to mentally work through things. He encouraged her to share her thoughts.

"Would there be any reason either brother might think *you* could be directly responsible for his disappearance? I mean,

59

considering Kaseem had so many enemies," she inquired.

"It's hard to say. My reaction in the courtroom after the verdict was publicized in the media. I was a bit emotional for a few minutes after they announced that Kaseem was not guilty. Of course, I didn't try to engage in physical, hand-to-hand combat or loud verbal threats because in spite of my feelings, I was sharply aware of the trigger-happy, armed, law enforcement personnel around me."

"Besides, my mother was already grieving and upset, and I didn't want to cause a scene or get arrested. But, I did struggle for a moment with my anger and walked closer to Kaseem ready to draw blood when I saw the sinister joy he had on his face and that he didn't feel an ounce of remorse for killing my sister."

Adara reflected on all the information Netar had shared. His reaction after the verdict was understandable. Walking away actually should detract suspicion from him. Everyone knows he doesn't have a history of violence and most people would see his actions as benign and a sign of surrender or letting go.

Furthermore, since there would be no physical evidence linking him to Kaseem's disappearance, his brothers would have no proof he was involved. People were more likely investigate the other potential suspects than Netar.

When she expressed that to Netar, he was impressed with her analysis of the situation. He agreed that he wouldn't likely be a suspect to the police or Kaseem's family. "It's a very slim chance that we will encounter any problems. I'm just trying to make sure we keep our eyes open. I feel obligated to protect you. The men I described have no conscience, Adara. They have brutalized and killed women, children and innocent people without remorse," he said while trying to avoid looking directly into Adara's eyes.

"So, we have to take every precaution possible. Listen, I want you to have my contact information," he said as he took out his wallet and gave Adara a card.

The card was completely black sans letters or any hint of symbols. Netar said, "I know it looks strange. The information on that card only shows when it's completely dark. The letters will glow, and you will be able to retrieve information that only a few, select people have."

"I ask that you not share it with anyone. I

recommend you go use one of the closets now to read the card. Put everything in your phone immediately which is another matter we need to talk about at a later time. And, make sure you keep the card hidden safely somewhere. Adara, I insist that you call me any time of day or night if you ever feel afraid. I mean it. Don't hesitate to contact me. Remember, I've made a promise to God to protect you forever," Netar reiterated.

The two sat silently for several minutes as Netar longingly searched Adara's face. They shared a tranquil moment as they reflected on what they'd discussed. They knew this single event would connect them for eternity. For several minutes Adara allowed herself to completely embrace Netar's intense inspection of her.

Each time she looked at his handsome, ebony skin and chiseled features, she was reminded of the ancient African warriors her grandmother had told her about as a child. His height made her think that he could be a direct descendent of the Nubian princes of Sudan or the Maasai from Kenya.

His intellect could have come from his ancestors of Timbuktu in Mali. His nobility and confidence were passed down by Shaka Zulu himself. His courage had flowed from the Nile and the powerful pharaohs of Egypt. He really was a combination of all these great men — he was their lost son of history, she thought with admiration.

While Adara was still a virgin and had never even kissed a man, she instinctively recognized that Netar was different. She had often watched men from afar. Until Netar had abruptly entered her life, it seemed that everything her grandmother had said about men was true. "They are dogs — two-legged snakes, Adara. All they want is one thing, and when they've had that, they leave as if you never existed."

When Adara started to become more physically developed around sixteen, she happily agreed to always cover her body as her grandmother had demanded. Adara didn't think wearing oversized clothing was unusual because most girls in her small, rural community were just as modest as she was.

However, when she came to college, she was shocked to see so many wantonly-dressed, young women. Their risqué attire seemed to reinforce all the lessons Adara's grandmother had taught. She observed how men objectified those women, used their bodies for pleasure, and tossed them away later as if they were like trash. She painfully witnessed so many young women cancel their dreams and hopes because they allowed men to misuse and abuse them.

It amazed Adara that many female students on campus saw themselves as victims of male chauvinism and misguided machismo rather than willing participants in their own maltreatment and demise. They faulted men instead of themselves for the lack of respect they endured.

Yet countless, young women walked down the street clothed like harlots soliciting men for prostitution. At the same time, they seemed totally surprised and offended when men gawked at their bodies and propositioned them for sex. Their tired complaint was that the only thing men seemed interested in was their bodies, but ironically that's all they seemed to be offering.

Using her classmates' lives as cautionary tales, during her sophomore year of college Adara vowed to God that she would never defile her body this way. In fact, she decided to never give herself to a man and become a nun after her grandmother died. Although she had heard and read about love between a man and women, she wasn't sure what that really meant.

For her, love was an illusion used in fabricated stories to entertain people. Yet somehow, she knew Netar was a real man capable of real love. He had made her start to rethink everything she believed. He possessed an intoxicating mystique — a je ne sais quoi that she did not understand. This frightened her, yet it awakened her senses at the same time. She knew she had to get away from him or she would succumb to the disturbing awakening that her body had never experienced before.

When Adara stood up to leave the kitchen, so did Netar. For each step he took forward, she stepped backwards. Eventually, she could no longer escape his advances and ended up against a wall.

Netar, towering over Adara's small stature, placed both of his strong arms easily on each side of her head. Realizing she was trapped, she looked at both of his powerful arms, but she did nothing to move away. Now weak and vulnerable to her newly discovered passions, her arms remained frozen to her sides while Netar leaned in closer. They were nearly touching and she became inebriated with his unique body scent and cologne. She inhaled deeply but made no effort to push him away.

"What have you done to me, little angel?" he seemed to be asking himself rather than Adara.

"I want to kiss you, but I know that I shouldn't — this isn't the right time for us," Netar continued with his intimate monologue.

"Ma chérie, tu es qui? Pourquoi tu as mon coeur si vite? Je ne peux pas arrêter mes sentiments pour toi," he whispered seductively in French.

Thankfully, before he did what both of them knew they would later regret, he placed a soft kiss on Adara's forehead and quickly left the room.

Three Nights in December

Chapter 10
Matters of the Heart

Netar couldn't believe he had walked away from Adara. His loins literally ached from unrequited desire, but somehow he'd managed to enclose himself in his bedroom to cool off and resist the urge to smoke a joint. When he'd promised God that he would protect her, he didn't realize it would have to be from himself.

As he rested comfortably in a large chaise, he remembered the wisdom of his dad had shared with him several years before. When he was in college his father had become concerned about his personal life. He didn't want Netar to end up like so many athletes with children born from their lust — children that those men would have a hard time loving because they didn't love their mothers — children that they wouldn't be able to support when their careers had ended, and they were financially broke with millions of dollars in debt and child support.

Netar's father knew as his son's football career began to grow, he'd have women constantly trying to seduce him. Many of those women would see him as a meal-ticket and by any means necessary, work to trap him by getting pregnant. He also knew that no matter how mentally or spiritually strong a man was he could easily succumb to sexual temptation.

Netar never forgot the call he received late one night. Anytime his father used the words, "we need to talk, son" he knew it was going to be serious. His father seemed to arrive to Florida so fast he hadn't a chance to tidy his dorm room. Impeccably dressed as usual, his father took him to a nearby restaurant and imparted life lessons that would inevitably spare Netar's life from disaster.

"Son, I am here to save your life," his father started. "I'm aware that you've been getting a lot of attention on and off the football field. Some of it's good, but most of it is dangerous. Nevertheless, I am extremely proud of you. You've always respected me, and your mother and we don't take your actions for granted. We have friends whose sons have already been to prison a few times. So, I thank God for His grace over your life, but there is so much more our Heavenly Father wants from you."

"Our faith requires that we be set apart from the world. On the other hand, people who have a worldly mindset believe in the concept of

Three Nights in December

'anything goes' which usually translates to mindlessly do *whatever* makes you feel good; and act on every physical impulse or emotion. This especially applies to the world's attitude about sex," he continued.

"I know you're a man, a healthy, sexually-wired human being. I also know you've already had sex and so far you've protected yourself from diseases and getting someone pregnant by using condoms. But while God has wired us with hormones that make us desire sex, He has also given us the ability to overcome our carnal cravings and impulses."

"Son, that's what separates us from animals. Netar, never forget that your mind is much more powerful than the manhood between your legs. I know it's hard. The Lord knows I understand because I am a man just as you are. But, I don't want you to ever think that your penis controls you and it's not the other way around. That's the life of weak men."

"Contrary to popular belief, a man doesn't have to roam the earth like a wild beast having sex with anyone or anything just because his hormones scream at him. Let me tell you, I've been tempted more times than I can count, but I have never cheated on your mother. I have had a thousand opportunities to do that, but I always saw the snares my spiritual enemy laid out for me. It doesn't matter how pretty it's packaged I know it's really rotten on the inside. In the end, satan can't trick a man who understands that one moment of pleasure is NOT worth a lifetime of pain."

"Through my own experiences, I am keenly aware that the mind is able to conjure up wicked thoughts. Netar, all wrongdoing first starts with a thought and the more you entertain that thought, the easier it becomes to act on it. And, it doesn't need help from extrinsic stimuli. That stuff, like the pornography so many men allow themselves to become enslaved to, only exacerbates the problem. Son, I strongly recommend you guard your heart and mind. You'll never be able to truly love a woman once the sexual filth and perversion like porn entraps your mind!" he added emphatically.

"People are not promoting loving a woman because they understand the flesh is weak. Plus, feeble-minded people can't love who they should and how they should. That requires a lot more spiritual energy and faith. But if you let your mind get entangled with what's not real—what's been fabricated by sick people to make money from weak men, you'll never be able to fully enjoy the essence of a woman—a woman that God created for you to love and cherish."

"In fact, God never intended for love and sex to be separated. Your desire of a woman should come from loving her, not lust. Trust me son, love is enough for you to enjoy her without the perversion of the world polluting your bedroom."

"Now look, Netar, I know I am lecturing," He lightly chuckled, "but to sum up in a nutshell what I am trying to say is that you must use your faith in order to resist and overcome temptation. You must be a disciplined man. These young women at this university will offer you all the desires your flesh can handle, but you must be careful. You must not ever put your seed in any woman you don't love."

Netar, always dutiful and respectful to his parents, had remained silent and attentive as his dad spoke. After the powerful lecture, he tried to fully digest his father's words as they sat speechless for a few minutes. He knew his dad deeply loved him and was inculcating the wisdom of God to protect him from avoidable trouble and pain. The evening continued with the two talking until the wee hours of the morning. Netar mostly listened though and tried to let the provocative words marinate in his mind. He never forgot how that long, father/son conversation became a pivotal moment in his life.

When Netar's father returned to New York, the young man committed to praying for several weeks about the direction his life should take. Finally, he decided that it was God's will that he give up football after college. He knew his own strengths and weaknesses and decided that life as a professional athlete would not be best for him. He didn't care that he disappointed quite a few fans when he didn't enter the NFL draft because he knew that the same men who admired him for his physical prowess, would never respect him as an intellectual.

In the end the only thing that mattered to Netar was that he was blessed to have a family that wholeheartedly supported his decision. He never regretted his choice to give up something that seemed innocuous but would have ultimately caused his demise. With his Bachelor of Science degree in Mechanical Engineering from the University of Florida, he had fared quite well.

Chapter 11
The Nun

After the "close call" with Netar, Adara chatted with her grandmother for a few minutes. Hearing her familiar voice sobered her mind a bit. Later, she had kept herself occupied by cleaning the kitchen, washing her clothing, and reading. Ivisse had given her a copy of J. California Cooper's book, *The Matter is Life* for Christmas and she hadn't been able to put it down. She was glad she'd kept the book in her backpack. She quickly became absorbed in the content and was relieved by the distraction from Netar who later found her curled up on his bed when he entered the bedroom.

"Hey," he greeted her smiling. "What do we have planned for dinner?"

"Well, I'm flexible. I don't mind cooking whatever you want," she said while placing the open book face down on the nightstand, giving him her full, undivided attention. "What do you have in the refrigerator?"

"Well, we've got steak, chicken, fish, pork chops… you name it. Just prepare whatever *you* want. I am totally impressed with your cooking. It's been a long time since I've had a good home-cooked meal."

"Thanks. I actually enjoy cooking. When I was around eight years old, my grandmother started teaching me how to cook. We rarely ate out because she believed that people couldn't control what was going in their bodies and they compromised their health when they let other people prepare their food. She always used to say that the more a person eats out, the more likely he or she will stay sick," Adara said.

"Good point," Netar said. "I guess when we say our good-byes I need to learn how to cook. By the way, I just got a new weather update and it seems the ice is finally melting. I'll probably be able to get you home tomorrow night," he said lightly.

"I just hope they've got the forecast right. The weather in Georgia is so unpredictable," Adara said as she started walking to the kitchen. "I can't wait to get back home," she added.

Netar sat silently for a few moments before responding to Adara's statement. He was enjoying watching her prepare their dinner. "Adara, I would like to ask you a few questions. I can only imagine how terrifying you probably feel being in the home of man you don't know, especially after what you've witnessed, but I want you to feel comfortable talking to me and being in my presence. If you think that I am prying, and you don't want to answer me, I will not be offended. I respect you so just let me know if you don't want to talk."

Adara was starting to feel more relaxed staying in Netar's house, but she wasn't sure how to interpret the tone of his voice. She no longer felt he would intentionally or maliciously hurt her, but she wondered what would happen if she offended him. She decided that there would be no harm in answering a few questions.

"I don't mind answering your questions," she said. All she hoped was that being compliant meant that Netar would release her as promised.

"Good. I only want to get to know you. That way we won't be strangers anymore. I keep saying that I will never hurt you, but I don't think you're convinced I'm telling the truth. So, I'll start with a confession. Kaseem had been stalking you. As I tried to keep track of his moves, I couldn't help becoming more intrigued with the object of his attention. I guess you can say that I was stalking you, too, but for good instead of evil."

Netar continued, "I don't think I'd ever seen a woman dressed like you. It's beyond modest. It's like you're purposely trying to hide your body from the world. Of course, I know women like to be dressed comfortably, but wearing something two sizes too big is a bit unusual," Netar said while greedily searching Adara's lovely face.

She felt his eyes sear hotly through her body and managed to answer without stuttering in spite of her nervousness, "Well, I like being conservative. I was taught that women shouldn't stir up lust and should cover themselves in public. I also believe that my body is sacred. Everyone shouldn't have access to it whether clothed or undressed," she said keeping her eyes on the food she was cooking.

"Of course, there's nothing wrong with how you dress. I just haven't seen many young women with your style. But I have to tell you that oversized clothing won't deter men from desiring you. Kaseem is a primary example. In fact, because you are so beautiful, Adara, it might peak a man's interest. Discovering what's underneath all those layers of material could become an enjoyable challenge for a man," Netar said seductively.

Netar couldn't help chuckling at the expression of confusion registering on Adara's face. "You appear not to know much about men.

Three Nights in December

Have you ever dated? I never saw you talk to any of your male classmates on campus even though quite a few tried to talk to you."

"No, I don't know much about men," Adara admitted truthfully. "I haven't ever dated. I didn't even go to prom in high school," she added.

"Wow. Was this by choice or forced by your parents?" Netar asked shocked.

"Well, first my parents are deceased. They died in a car accident," she said solemnly. "I've been raised by my maternal grandmother since I was eight years old."

Adara took a deep breath. A myriad of emotions could surface whenever she spoke of her mother and father.

"I am sorry to hear about your loss," Netar said sincerely. "Do you have any siblings?"

"No, I am an only child like my father was. But, I have an aunt who lives in California. Fina is my mother's sister and she's married to Chandler, which makes him my uncle. They have two children so at least I have cousins, Senghor and Martin. It's sad that I just don't get to see them often because they live so far away, and it costs so much for them to travel."

C. Chérie Hardy

"To answer your other question, my grandmother never said I couldn't date, but I had never asked her either," Adara said.

"So, are you telling me you're a virgin?" Netar asked in a low voice.

Adara paused for several moments. She had started to become uncomfortable with the topic of discussion. Hesitating she said, "Yes, I am a virgin. I've pledged to give my life to God. When my grandmother dies, I will become a nun. I will be spiritually married to Christ," she finished.

"What? Wait! Did you say the word, *nun*?" Netar said with a hint of laughter in his voice. "Adara, you truly are different! I hope you don't mind me saying this, but you'd make a terrible nun. I'm not trying to put you down, but you could do so much more for God's kingdom as a wife and a mother."

"Furthermore, you are far too beautiful. I am not trying to insult the good sisters, but you would stand out like a rose on a cactus plant in that homely bunch. I can just imagine you having to fight off horny priests and other nuns every day," he added shaking his head and trying not to burst out laughing.

Three Nights in December

Adara looked totally astounded by his last comment. Netar sensed that she hadn't thought about the dark side of the church. "I have to ask, what *really* made you decide to become a nun, Adara? Why are you trying to avoid interaction with men? What is the underlying reason you're pledging your life to eternal virginity? It just seems so extreme. Inquiring minds must get the answer today," Netar said playfully.

Adara hesitated, not sure if she could handle Netar ridiculing her thoughts. "I...well... If you really want to know the truth, I have been taught that men are like thoughtless beasts. They use you for your body like meat and toss you away like bones when they've gotten full from lust. I became convinced that the best way not to get hurt by men is to stay away from them. A monastery seemed like the perfect place for a woman to hide," she responded.

Netar was pensive for a moment. He could see that dinner was almost ready. Choosing his words carefully he said, "Adara, there is no place on the planet a person can hide from pain. In spite of our faith and good intentions and actions, we get hurt. Sometimes, we even unintentionally hurt others. Do you know you could get hurt as a nun?"

"My grandfather used to say that pain is an integral part of life. And, that all pain has a purpose. You just have to look for the treasures buried beneath life's trials and tribulations. My sweet angel, it's inevitable that every human being will suffer some variation of the same pain. We lose; we gain. We give; we take. We live; we die. I could go on. Pain is going to be there, and we have to learn how to endure it — learn from it — become wiser and stronger because of it. The truth is you can run from pain, but you just can't hide. Yes, a man could hurt you. I'd be lying if I didn't say that. However, there are countless men who wouldn't, not on purpose. They could love and protect you as if their life depended upon it. But, even those men aren't going to be perfect. They will make mistakes as all humans do. A man with a good heart will grow and learn from his mistakes; he'll strive be a better person because of his relationship with you — a gift from God to be treasured," Netar ended.

Adara looked at Netar and said, "Thank you. All I can say is 'touché'. I appreciate you helping me see things from another perspective. I know your words came from God. I realize now that faith and fear can't dwell in my heart at the same time. There can't be fear in love. I'll just have to trust God and let Him purge my mind of all the negative thoughts I have concerning men. And, I guess I won't become a nun after all," she whispered.

"No, you will not," Netar answered as if he was a seasoned soothsayer. He then walked over to Adara and held her for a few moments. It was the first time they had embraced. He allowed himself to fully share a sacred, spiritual transference of emotion with Adara.

In the core of his spirit, he knew that God had now bonded their hearts. It seemed every cell in his body was screaming for him to kiss her, but he didn't. Netar kept thinking how good he felt just holding Adara. He didn't let go until she whispered that she needed to turn off the stove. Neither spoke until dinner was finished.

"If you will let me, I would like to demonstrate how a good man should treat you," Netar said interrupting the silence.

"I'm not asking you to give me your heart until I've proven that I deserve it. I want to earn your trust and respect. I hate we met under these unfortunate circumstances, but how our story ends will be much sweeter than its beginning. Will you let me show you love?" Netar asked as he walked towards Adara.

This time Adara didn't back away as Netar approached her. In fact, she closed her eyes and welcomed his embrace. They held each other for what seemed like an eternity. She knew that Netar was waiting for her answer.

"Yes, I will let you show me love," Adara said softly.

"Merci, chérie. Je te désire et je t'aime toujours," Netar responded before making sure Adara would never forget her first kiss.

Chapter 12
Business

After dinner, Netar decided to make a few important telephone calls before spending more time talking to Adara. He spoke to his parents and brother and assured them he was coming home for Christmas. He also contacted Fitz, whose full name was Fitzgerald Thomas, the lead manager of his company, to see how things were going. He knew that Fitz was trustworthy and would take care of things with integrity while he was away from the business. Fitz's loyalty had been sealed when Netar hired him in spite of his criminal record.

Netar had met Fitz after the trial. Initially, he had returned to New York with his family. His primary concern was the mental and emotional health of his mother. Once he was confident his mother was okay, he decided to relocate to Atlanta. At some point, he was offered an engineering job with Lockheed Martin and had almost signed his contract when his uncle convinced him to open a franchise of the family's heating and air business.

His uncle, Charles was convinced that this was the kind of more physically-demanding work that Netar needed to keep him out of trouble. Furthermore, starting the franchise would be creating a legacy for the Moore family. Netar reluctantly agreed, but after his uncle set up things, organized a complete training program and business model, Netar began to love the work.

Uncle Charles designed the hiring protocols and encouraged Netar to consider men who needed a second chance. Uncle Charles, a former felon, knew that with the right knowledge and opportunities, even men with a criminal history could transform their lives and become model citizens of their communities. He acknowledged that *all* men were not humble, open-minded, and teachable enough to be rehabilitated. However, those who were would never get a second chance without privately-owned businesses that cared more about healing men than repeatedly punishing them for the mistakes they had made.

Uncle Charles also knew men needed to be taught discipline and work ethic because many of them had grown up without fathers and positive male role models. He had met many guys who had resorted to a life of crime because they didn't know *how* to do better. They grew up in a crime-ridden, drug-infested and economically impoverished communities where life was about survival of the fittest. Everybody was competing for a limited amount of resources and people resorted to extreme measures to reduce their suffering. Uncle Charles did not make excuses for people, but he understood the concept of cause and effect.

With this in mind, Uncle Charles created a comprehensive employee plan for the business that included both personal and professional development as a surefire way to reduce the recidivist rate. Netar would never forget the day when Fitz entered his office for an interview. Uncle Charles interrogated him mainly about his personal and social habits as well as his mindset to determine if he really wanted to abandon a life in the streets.

Fitz met the profile of a male who had gotten on the wrong side of the law as a way of survival. His heart was good. He was also eager to learn and yearned for a second chance. He just needed someone to show him what to do.

Uncle Charles was personally familiar with Fitz's plight. As a teenager he had started socializing with a bad crowd. It wasn't a long time before he ended up being convicted as an

C. Chérie Hardy

accessory to armed robbery and spent three
years in a New York prison. When he was
released, he had tried desperately to get a job
and support himself, but every door had been
slammed in his face because of his criminal
record. He also knew that as a Black man he
wouldn't be forgiven for his transgressions by
mainstream society.

Thank God his father, Netar's
grandfather, believed in self-reliance.
Grandfather believed that men were a product
of choice, not genetics, circumstances, and
chance. At the same time, he understood that
some people didn't *know* that they possessed the
God-given ability to make their own choices.

Without wisdom, they would maintain a
mindset of victimhood, always thinking their
problems were a result of someone else's actions.
Grandfather, having had survived so much evil
throughout his life had learned the formula for
success — we create the life we want by changing
our minds — how we mentally see things.

Changing our thoughts leads to the
transformation of our actions, but people need
encouragement, education, and economic
support. But, the most important lesson of all
was that the objective in life was not to get, it

was to keep. And the only way a man could keep what he gained was through integrity. So, Grandfather and his brothers spent weeks talking and planning about how they could not only help Charles turn his life around, and other men in the community who had endured the same fate.

Eventually the family agreed to start a heating and air service. After putting their resources together, it wasn't long before they had hired and trained other young men like Charles about how to live a righteous life that involved hard work, respect and taking care of one's family. What mattered though is that these men had the economic resources to meet their needs.

When Fitz was offered the job, Netar remembered him repeating the question, "Man, are you serious?" He must have said that at least ten times before leaving the office. Now, Fitz leads twenty other men at the company. Most have the same background as Fitz. The model of personal transformation Uncle Charles taught him is what he teaches to new employees of the company. This is what allowed Netar to be away for a few days to shelter his angel, Adara.

Chapter 13
Loyalty

Netar felt he could no longer delay disposing the items he'd taken from Kaseem's car. He hated bringing them to his house, but it was the only way he could be certain they would never be found. He quickly got the fireplace going in the living room. He could use the fire to destroy any incriminating evidence, but also he wanted to create a cozy ambiance for the time he planned to continue talking to Adara.

He had stashed the bag behind some firewood adjacent to the master bedroom's patio. First, he carefully unloaded the gun and took out the knife. He planned to chop them up and distribute the parts in various regions of the city. He discovered five thousand dollars cash in an envelope which he quickly deduced were the ill-gotten gains resulting from Kaseem's various criminal enterprises. He'd give all of the money to a women's homeless shelter after he returned Adara to her apartment.

Lastly, he took out Kaseem's wallet. Touching it made him feel nauseous. He removed Kaseem's driver's license, social security card and a few other miscellaneous documents that he would shred and later put in the fire. As he skimmed over the papers, he found a small, tightly-folded, gold-colored note. His heart did a somersault when he saw Adara's name, apartment number and phone number written in a handwriting that looked too feminine to be Kaseem's.

After recovering from a few minutes of shock, he tried to imagine how Kaseem got this information. He would be surprised as well as devastated to know Adara had voluntarily given him her personal information. During the time he spent studying her habits, he'd seen her refuse to even look at Kaseem. He'd talk to her about it later, but something about his discovery unsettled him.

He shredded all the documents, as well as Kaseem's wallet which he later tossed in his fireplace. In his back yard, he chopped up the Kaseem's weapons and bagged them for future disposal. As he worked, he couldn't stop thinking about the gold-colored note.

After he'd put everything in the fireplace, he walked to Adara's bedroom. Once again, he found her reading. She seemed so content that he hated interrupting her. Smiling and trying not to appear worried, he said, "Adara, I just found something in Kaseem's wallet that you need to know about. Please come in the living room so we can talk."

Adara recognized something alarming in Netar's tone and mannerisms, but she told herself to stay calm. She slowly walked in the living room and sat down on the loveseat facing the sofa where Netar was sitting.

Looking directly into Adara's eyes he said, "I need you to be totally truthful about what I am going to ask you. This could be a matter of life and death. Think carefully and tell me if you ever remember giving Kaseem your phone and apartment number," Netar said calmly.

"There is no way I would have ever given my number to Kaseem. Someone could have offered me a million dollars to do so and I would have refused. Each time he tried to talk to me, I ignored him and walked away. Did he have my number?" she asked puzzled.

"I found this in his wallet." Netar said and handed Adara the gold-colored note. Immediately, when she saw the writing she stood up, covered her mouth and repeated about four times, "Oh my God!"

"What is it?" Netar said standing up, too.

Three Nights in December

"Netar, I recognize this handwriting. It's Ivisse's, my friend and co-worker from the library. No way! She must have given this to Kaseem! Wait! Let me show you something."

Adara quickly got the book that Ivisse had given to her for Christmas. Ivisse had signed on the dedication page, "To my best friend, Adara, may you have a beautiful holiday filled with love."

Netar studied both documents and realized that the handwriting matched. Suddenly, he remembered seeing Ivisse walking alone with Kaseem one day. He didn't think it was interesting or suspicious until now. "Do you think that Ivisse could have been seeing Kaseem and didn't tell you since he had been trying to ask you out first? Even though she knew you didn't like him she could have thought she'd lose her friendship with you if she revealed she was dating him."

"It's possible Netar, but…I just can't believe this. I am so shocked right now. Ivisse never mentioned Kaseem whenever we talked. She always said she thought he was a creep as I had."

"Has Ivisse tried to contact you recently?" Netar asked.

"Yes. Wait, oh my!" Adara said with a befuddled look on her face. "You know, she has called me two days in a row. Even though that's not unusual, she knows I only have a prepaid phone and rarely make social calls. As I reflect on it now, she sounded strange."

"In fact, when we spoke this morning, she seemed like she had been crying. She asked me about my location and plans for the holiday which was weird because I had already shared my plans with her before she left. Nevertheless, I just told her again that I couldn't travel to North Carolina because of finances and I would spend the break reading in my apartment."

"Netar, what if Ivisse had expected to hear from Kaseem and since she hasn't she's become curious and/or worried about his whereabouts?"

The idea that Ivisse and Kaseem could have had a clandestine relationship right under her nose floored Adara. She had considered Ivisse her best friend, but now she didn't know how to think.

"Do you think Ivisse would contact the police and report Kaseem missing?" Adara asked.

Netar stood silently and tried to think. A

person didn't have to be a psychologist to know that human behavior was always unpredictable.

"We can never be too sure." He paused for a few minutes before adding," Well, this is a good segue to something I have wanted to tell you since yesterday," he said as Adara sat down on the loveseat.

"You have become very special to me, Adara. Although it will take every fiber of my being to stay away from you, we cannot see each other for months or maybe years until I am sure that you're safe and no one connects me to Kaseem's disappearance. Association with me is too dangerous for you right now, but I want you to know that I am completely enchanted by you. Please consider allowing me to properly court you when the time is safe."

Adara kept her head down while allowing Netar's words to permeate her spirit. She felt she'd melt if she looked into Netar's eyes. Intuitively, she knew that whatever she felt for Netar was beyond her control. She had not chosen Netar. God had placed him in her life. With her naïveté and mis-education about men, she could not have possibly even imagined that a man like Netar existed. God, in His infinite wisdom had brought her and Netar together.

C. Chérie Hardy

She knew that Netar was right about the hiatus they would have to endure. But, it was going to be hard because she became more attached to him as they shared more time together. She chuckled inwardly thinking how strange it was that she had once thought of becoming a nun.

Obviously, God had other plans. She lifted her head and smiled. They both stood up and Netar completely surrendered to the sweet beckoning of her soft, voluptuous lips. Adara thought that her second kiss seemed as long and wide as her emotions for Netar. It was perfect, and she never wanted it to end.

Three Nights in Decmeber

Chapter 14
Au Revoir

Netar tried to make his last day with Adara as special as possible. After they cooked and ate breakfast together, he engaged her in a few rounds of Scrabble, Adara's favorite board game. After losing every round, Netar taught her how to play chess. He was impressed with Adara's calculation and analyzing skills. He could certainly see that she had the potential to become a good player.

Of course, she was no match for a chess master, but he allowed her to win a match before beating her, hoping she wouldn't lose her confidence. She was an apt student as he explained the strategies and visualization he used and why. One day, he thought, she might be able to defeat him.

Adara insisted on preparing a big dinner for them which they enjoyed by candlelight in front of the fireplace. She and Netar laughed and talked about everything, including controversial topics like politics, sex, religion and money. He liked that they could disagree with mutual respect.

C. Chérie Hardy

Adara admired that Netar was an oratory wordsmith who eagerly listened to her ideas. Netar's openness, honesty and amiable personality created a bonhomous atmosphere that made her comfortable sharing some of her most intimate thoughts. They discovered that although they had grown up in different, geographical parts of the country, they had been raised with similar values about many issues.

When Adara asked why he hadn't married yet, it was so easy for him to answer, but he decided to share a childhood story he had been told many times. "You know, angel," Netar started, "I feel fortunate to have had good examples of loving and successful Black men in my life. They instilled in me from a very early age that the woman I chose could have a direct effect on the outcome and quality of my life. My grandfather used to reiterate that the woman in a man's life could make it seem like hell or paradise on earth. He would often tell a powerful story to illustrate this point."

"He said he once befriended two men who grew up in the same neighborhood with similar backgrounds. One man thought his manhood was determined by the *quantity* of women he could get in his bed. He was driven by distorted machismo, lust, and selfishness. On the other hand, the second man learned that a good life could be created by the *quality* of the woman he chose."

"The latter man began to search for *one* good woman. Eventually he found a woman who was a reflection of his own good heart. He wasn't intimidated by her strength and intelligence, but in fact, appreciated and admired those things in her. In the end, the second man lived longer; looked better; had more; and was happier than the first," Netar said pausing for a moment to study Adara's lovely face.

"That's why I haven't married yet. I had never felt a cerebral connection with a woman until I met you. I always knew that when I had met the right woman, I'd want to make passionate love to her mind before I had ever touched her body. I also desired someone who had a serious spiritual life. That's what makes you so adorable, Adara. Ma belle chérie, your mind and heart are just as beautiful as you are physically," Netar said with a winsome smile that made Adara's heart dance.

The finale to their romantic evening consisted of Netar opening the drawer to the end table and pulling out a poetry book. "I want to read to you," he announced alluringly.

They sat closely to each other with Netar's arm protectively around Adara's shoulder. He started with Shakespeare's, "Shall I Compare Thee to a Summer Day" and continued with e. e. cummings's poem, "somewhere I have never traveled, gladly beyond".

Adara closed her eyes and imagined herself and Netar had transcended in an Elysium field of bliss and preternatural love. When Netar read the last poem, "At Last" by Elizabeth Akers Allen, Adara felt the wave of emotion ascend from her heart to her tear ducts. She managed though not to release a single tear.

Netar just held her as if he'd die if he let go. "This is our last night together, ma chérie – at least for some time. It's sad to know that it's time to say, 'au revoir', my angel. I'll hate it as much as you will, but I know that it's best for us to keep a distance until I am absolutely sure you're safe. When I know that no one is looking for Kaseem and people have moved on, we will be together. We'll go wherever you want, and do whatever you want, my angel," Netar said.

"But, if you ever feel threatened, call me. Whether it is by phone or via your heart reach out to me and I promise I'll protect you. Just remember that I'll still be around looking over you, but our relationship can't be public until the time is right."

"Lastly, I have a few Christmas gifts for you. First, I want to make sure you get all the grocery your refrigerator and cupboards can hold before dropping you off tomorrow. Also, if you really want to fly up to North Carolina to see your grandmother, I will get the ticket. I'll give you the cash and drop you off at the airport. And one more thing, I have a card for you, but I don't want you to open it until Christmas day."

"Netar, you are so thoughtful. I can't thank God enough for bringing you into my life. I truly appreciate you," Adara said as she tightened their embrace.

That night Netar and Adara fervently prayed together before falling asleep cuddled in the each other's arms.

Chapter 15
Christmas

Three days before Christmas Netar returned Adara to her apartment. She had accepted his generous gift of unlimited grocery and household supplies. However, she decided not to go home for the holiday. As much as she cherished her grandmother and wanted to see her, she was not ready to reveal aspects of her newly discovered womanhood. She was acutely aware that Netar's presence in her life had created both subtle and overt changes in the way she walked, talked and thought.

While they had not consummated their spiritual marriage, she had been physically awakened by passions that she never even imagined existed. For some reason, Adara thought her grandmother would look through her and sense that she was no longer an innocent girl who aspired to become a nun. Adara simply wasn't ready to share that special part of her life with anyone, not even her beloved grandmother. Moreover, she didn't think her grandmother would understand the love Adara had for Netar.

In the past her grandmother had continually spoken about her abhorrence for men. However, it was greater, spiritual hindsight that helped Adara to realize that her grandmother had unintentionally projected her personal, negative experiences about relationships onto her life. She inferred that her grandmother had been so hurt by a man that she had closed her heart forever to love.

Adara felt a deep sadness knowing that the woman who had raised her possessed so much love to give yet had never found someone to fully embrace her beautiful heart. Despite the fact that her grandmother was in her mid-sixties, Adara prayed that it wasn't too late for the kindhearted woman. She stood in faith for her grandmother knowing that with God all things are possible.

As Adara pondered over how her life had drastically changed in three nights with Netar, questions bombarded her mind. There was so much she had to sort through mentally. She desperately missed Netar, but what if her impression of him was wrong. She had learned a long time ago that patience was one of the most effective, personal security systems. It was always wise to look beyond your initial ideas about an issue or a person.

Yet each time memories of Netar surfaced

in her mind, she felt a sense of peace. Just as she thought of him, she remembered the bright red envelope he'd handed her before saying good-bye. She took it out and gently stroked her fingers across its creases but kept her promise not to open it until Christmas day. She thanked God that Netar had not taken advantage of her physical and emotional vulnerability; a lesser man would have not been so sensitive and patient.

He must have known that she would find it hard to forgive herself for being weak, and not using her faith to rise above her passions. Netar was technically a stranger to her. He knew she would have felt self-induced guilt and condemnation if she had given away her body which she considered a sacred temple.

The most poignant lesson she learned was that no matter how spiritual a person became, he or she was still flesh and blood and susceptible to succumbing to temptation. She remembered the scripture where Jesus encouraged his disciples to watch and pray because while the spirit was willing to do right, the flesh was weak. She finally understood exactly what that meant.

Three Nights in December

Furthermore, the heart could be fickle. What if ten months from now she still wanted to become a nun? What if Netar had changed his mind about her? He professed his love and had demonstrated with his actions that he cared, but people changed abruptly all the time. She was grateful for the break because she would have a little time to calm the rapidly firing storm of thoughts that were darting around in her mind.

Netar had been thinking of Adara, too. Hoping to avoid the hectic atmosphere of the country's busiest airport, he got a flight to New York as late as he could. He quickly discovered that red-eye flights around Christmas were just as crowded as other times. Grateful that the snow in New York hadn't delayed his trip, he was able to do some quick shopping for his nephews who were not old enough to understand why their uncle was coming home empty-handed.

Somehow Netar managed to navigate around the throngs of hyper shoppers and purchased three IPods, one for each boy. To get something special for his mother, he headed north and stopped by Robert Mills & Company Jewelry Store. The establishment was much quieter than expected as customers, namely giddy couples, seemed to whisper and glide around with a hushed kind of holiday cheer.

After trying to slyly peruse his clothing, one of the saleswomen offered her help. Netar expressed that he was looking for a unique piece with a peridot, his mother's birthstone. The woman plastered the most sincere-looking smile she could on her face, and led him to a small, private gallery on the other end of the building. Waving her hand as if she was Vanna White, she said, "Just let me know if you would like to look at anything," she said before going to another customer.

With probably fifty different colored rocks to choose from, Netar finally saw something to match his mother's conservative taste. It was a simple design: a two-carat, princess-cut stone surrounded by tiny pearls. He smiled as he pictured her joy when she opened the gift.

Now with the shopping done, he could get to his hotel room, shower and take a power-nap before heading to his parents' home. As he walked through the busy streets, thoughts of Adara warmed him. Everything about her clearly lingered in his mind which made the people around him appear like a blur. Their

Three Nights in December

three nights locked away together brought a whole new meaning to the expression, "cabin fever". Netar just kept visualizing the moment when he could just take out his phone and tell her something sweet or invoke her infectious laugh with a private joke.

Netar told himself that Adara might not be a gift he would have wrapped under the Christmas tree this year, but she would be the most memorable and cherished of all. He considered her a special blessing from God. He quietly prayed that she would accept his offer to become his wife. Imagining her as his *helpmate*, the one to warm his cold summers and represent peace during the tumultuous storms of life, made him smile. He knew that with patience and hope in God, the strange fate that forbade them to be together at this moment, would later unite them forever.

Whoever said absence makes the heart grow fonder was right. The more time Netar spent away from Adara, the more he desired her. At midnight on Christmas morning, through the telepathy of love, Netar and Adara stared at the brightest star in the sky. Space was of no consequence as they felt just as close as if they were in each other's arms.

Chapter 16
Ivisse

The first time Adara saw Ivisse after the break, she couldn't help noticing the drastic change in her physical countenance. Her eyes appeared tired and sunken in her once round face. Ivisse also seemed a bit distant each time she tried to engage her in a conversation. Finally, one evening after work, Ivisse asked Adara if she had heard from Kaseem. It had been about one month since his disappearance, but nothing had been reported in the news.

"Who is Kaseem?" Adara asked looking puzzled and directly in her friend's troubled eyes. "Who is that?"

"You know, the guy who used to meet us at the bus stop sometimes and chat with us when we left class," Ivisse responded.

Adara paused, feigning amnesia. "I don't remember him. Oh… now I know. Wasn't that the guy who harassed us? Why would I have heard from him? I wouldn't have talked to that creep if someone offered me a million bucks! He was a real jerk if you asked me. Why was he following us around instead of going to work or taking care of his family?" Adara exclaimed.

Three Nights in December

Ivisse couldn't hide her offense. "Well, while he wasn't good enough for you, Adara, aka Miss Goody Two Shoes, he seemed like a really nice guy to me. I saw his actions as determined, not bothersome."

"In fact," she hesitated for a few moments, "I went out with him a few times."

"What?" Adara said genuinely surprised by Ivisse's confession. "I didn't know you were dating him," Adara said truthfully.

"Yes. And, he treated me very well, Adara. He wasn't a creep to me! But, I haven't heard from him in weeks and I am worried. He was supposed to call me during the break," Ivisse said sadly. Her eyes became watery, then she continued, "I know you won't approve of what I am about to share, as you are so holier than thou," she said sarcastically, "but I even had sex with him."

Adara was momentarily speechless and let a wave of silence permeate the air. She reached out to hug her friend who immediately started sobbing so fiercely that her body shook. Adara reached into her purse, got some tissue and offered it to Ivisse. "Everything is going to be alright," she said trying to comfort her friend.

"It's possible he lost his phone and

misplaced your number by mistake. It happens all the time. I'm sure that he'll call you soon. Also, we've been away for almost a month. He might not have had a way to find out if you had returned from California. I'm sure he'll show up at any moment," Adara said with a performance that was worthy of an Oscar.

"Everything will be alright, Ivisse," Adara continued while patting her back. "I'm curious. What happens when you try to reach him? What kind of recording or message do you get?"

Ivisse's eyes were completely red as she responded, "At first, it would go to voicemail and I would leave a message. Now, the recording says that his mailbox is full and cannot take any more messages. I am starting to think that something happened to him. I have even considered going to the police. I have checked the news online to see if his name has come up, but nothing has."

Adara tried not to become alarmed when Ivisse mentioned the word, *police*. As long as law enforcement or his family was not looking for him, there would be no suspicion regarding his absence. "Ivisse, did you ever meet Kaseem's family? Is there someone you can contact who might be able to tell you something?" Adara said trying to gage just how much her classmate knew.

"No, I didn't. He mentioned that he had two brothers a few times, but I never met them. Kaseem had promised that when I returned to campus after the holiday, he was going to introduce me to everybody."

Just as Adara was wondering if Ivisse had considered Kaseem could have dumped her, she interrupted her thoughts. "If he got tired of me and wanted to end the relationship, all he had to do was call and tell me," she said recommencing her crying.

"But everything seemed to be going well. We hadn't even had an argument."

Adara just listened hoping Ivisse would accept that she had been dumped and move on. "Well, sometimes things work out for the best. If God wants you to be with Kaseem, you will. If not, he will have someone better come into your life. You are beautiful, intelligent and so kind. Someone will appreciate that, and no doubt help you move forward. Furthermore, we graduate in less than four months. Focusing on your classes and future plans might just ease your mind."

Ivisse reflected on Adara's words. "I just

wish I had closure. I want to know if he dumped me or if he's okay. I just wish I knew the truth."

"I am sure that if he's missing his family will contact the police," Adara said.

"I have even called the hospitals and the morgue, but it all led to nothing," Ivisse added.

"Well, why don't you let me treat you to dinner? This is a perfect time to indulge in some good soul food."

Ivisse laughed and accepted Adara's suggestion. The two of them talked about their classes as they walked to a nearby restaurant. It was a Wednesday evening and not as crowded as usual, so they didn't have to wait long for their food.

After about an hour, Adara excused herself from the table and headed for the restroom. She didn't think twice about leaving her purse in the chair with Ivisse. As soon as she left though, Ivisse rummaged through Adara's purse. Ivisse had suspected that somehow Adara was connected to Kaseem's inexplicable disappearance. She couldn't help noticing the large red envelope and immediately she pulled it out.

While the card was unsigned, she found a romantic letter inside that had been typed in a fancy font. She read it thoroughly and quickly placed it back in Adara purse, but her mind exploded with hate.

So Kaseem has been seeing Adara. No wonder she was encouraging me to move on and seemed totally unconcerned about his disappearance. That conniving witch! She knew exactly where Kaseem has been – with her! Who else could have typed that letter? To think that I actually believed that Adara was a virgin when she was sleeping with Kaseem!

While I was out in California with my family, Adara was charming my man. After all, he always wanted her – he always inquired about her. Damn! I had even given him her number. I cannot believe I was such a fool!

But, that's okay because they are going to wish they never betrayed me. I am going to make sure that the both of them pay dearly for this. I promise I will be the one to get the last laugh.

When Adara returned to the table she felt something foul in the air. She looked at Ivisse and could tell she was disturbed. "Is everything okay, Ivisse?" she asked.

"Yes, Adara, I am fine, but I would like to get back to my room and work on assignments that are due this week," Ivisse said tartly.

"Okay. You see, the soul food has already gotten you focused again," Adara said lightly trying to change Ivisse's mood.

"It surely has. Let's go!"

On the way back, the young women hardly talked. Each time Adara attempted to engage Ivisse in a conversation, she responded with a curt, impersonal response. It was clear that her sadness had transformed into anger, but Adara couldn't figure out why.

The dark spirit that now possessed Ivisse was almost tangible. Adara wanted to be supportive, but she became so disquieted about her friend's declining mental health that she couldn't wait to get away from her. Arriving to campus, they headed in opposite directions. When Adara tried to say, good-bye, Ivisse just snarled and walked away.

Chapter 17
Band of Brothers

Samuel was starting to feel uneasy about his brother's MIA status. While it wasn't unusual for Kaseem to go on some secret retreat and return without an explanation, a month was way too long. As each day came and went though, he expected Kaseem to pop up, appearing invigorated from some wicked adventure as he had many times in the past.

Kaseem was the brains while Samuel was the brawn of their enterprises. Kaseem organized and commanded how things worked. He was just a lieutenant, an enforcer of whatever Kaseem dictated. Normally, whenever Kaseem went on one of his special retreats, he would call Samuel after several days to check in on the business and inform him when he was returning. So when this didn't happen, Samuel started to have the sinking feeling that his brother had finally run into foul play. He knew that there was a long list of people who wished that Kaseem was dead and it was only a matter of time that their dreams would come true.

For many months, Samuel had been haunted by the words of Mr. Townsend, whose

113

wife Kaseem had brutally assaulted. Allegedly, the older woman had accidently stepped on his foot as she walked home from a neighborhood grocer. Samuel had replayed the terrible event in his head countless times. After learning about his beloved wife's misfortune, Mr. Townsend, walleyed and looking deranged, stormed down his stairs and confronted Kaseem.

Although he was whispering, his words seemed to thunder through the night's air. "God is going to punish you for all the evil you've done in this neighborhood," Mr. Townsend said with his voice filled with anguish. Although Kaseem tried to ignore him, the man boldly stood in Kaseem's face and continued, "When you die, all the souls of the people you beat, killed, raped, robbed and terrorized are going to torment your soul to eternity!"

Like a poisonous viper in a jungle, Kaseem responded by spitting in the old man's face. The helpless man just took out his handkerchief as his hands shook from the onset of Parkinson's disease, wiped the venom away and returned to his distraught wife. Spectators shook their heads that night, but no one dared to say anything because they feared Kaseem.

Everyone knew that Kaseem didn't just

kill. No, he specialized in torturing and maiming his victims to leave his evil signature on every noxious deed he committed. But, after that malicious act to Mr. Townsend and his wife, people began to loathe Kaseem so much that they prayed daily for his death. His name became utterly reviled by the young and old in the neighborhood.

His single vile incident was like the straw that broke the camel's back because Kaseem had violated a well-understood code of ethics, even for thugs: don't hurt the very young; innocent; and especially never bother the elderly.

While Samuel didn't interfere that night, he hated what had happened to Mr. Townsend and his wife. He had always respected the elderly gentleman and admired his humility because he saw how hard he worked to provide for his family. When Samuel and his brothers were growing up, they'd watch Mr. Townsend collect aluminum cans and other scrap metals. The man would ride an adult tricycle around with the stuff packed in a large basket behind him.

Often Samuel's friends would taunt Mr. Townsend, and the most vicious ones would throw rocks at the good man. But, Samuel remembered Mr. Townsend always trying to teach young boys how to do right. For the two or three boys who would listen, he would often reiterate that a real man isn't afraid of hard work. He would emphatically exclaim that he'd rather die instead of resorting to polluting the neighborhood with violence, sexual perversion and drugs. While many kids laughed at Mr. Townsend, Samuel took in his words. His wisdom had resonated with him throughout the years.

He felt so ashamed about what Kaseem had done that one day he secretly placed one thousand dollars in Mr. Townsend's mailbox. He wrote on the envelope, "I am sorry about what Kaseem did. You're a good man, Mr. Townsend and I respect you. Please forgive me."

Now that Kaseem was missing Samuel wondered if Mr. Townsend had killed his brother, but he didn't care. The thought that Kaseem might be dead actually gave him some relief. He loved his brother, but he was tired of their awful, Godless life. He didn't want more innocent people to be hurt or killed. He was sick of doing evil in the name of street justice. He was exhausted from never really getting a good night's sleep because as the eldest, he always had to look over his shoulder and protect his younger brothers, Kaseem and Jason. Everyone knew what he and his brothers did, and that made them targets for rival groups. Someone was constantly talking about taking Kaseem out because he was *too evil*.

Moreover, Samuel had never been able to reconcile his sister's suspicious death. Although he didn't have concrete evidence that Kaseem was responsible, everything hinted to his modus operandi. He hated to admit it, but his brother had mutated into a monster and maniac. There was only a remnant of humanity left in him. It was already bad that Kaseem had raped and killed an innocent, college student, but killing someone who shared his DNA was unfathomable — unforgivable. Samuel wished he knew how he could help heal his brother's rotten heart, but he felt Kaseem had become incorrigible and had reached a point of no return.

Samuel also knew that Kaseem would never let him voluntarily walk away from their business even with his six kids. He had been contemplating the idea for a few years and finally decided to share his plans with Kaseem. However, his brother thought it was ridiculous

117

that he wanted to spend his time focusing on fatherhood instead of attaining money and power through corruption and crime. Kaseem had called him a wimp and a fool for letting his heart grow soft for women and children.

After Kaseem's response, Samuel concluded that his brother was the most selfish and thoughtless human being he had ever known. He deeply regretted all the times he had rationalized Kaseem's behavior because of the abusive childhood they suffered.

Samuel had always blamed himself for not being able to protect Kaseem from the vile, sick things his sadist stepfather had done to them. When he was fourteen years old though, Samuel got the courage to slit his stepfather's throat. Unfortunately, the damage had already been done. Each member of the household developed his or her own way of coping with the haunting memories that became an integral part of their daily lives.

Thank God their baby sister, Yazmine had been born after their stepfather's death, and had escaped their torment. His mother however, consumed with guilt and self-loathing, was eventually committed to a mental health facility and later died there after seven years. To a certain extent all three brothers had become desensitized to violence, but Kaseem who had been the main target of their stepfather's evil, had become totally numb to it. It was like he made it his lifelong mission to hurt people because he had been.

Samuel believed that Kaseem created a façade of control and pseudo-strength in an effort to mask his feelings of powerlessness and disgust. In the same manner, he felt that he had to go to extremes to make people fear him. He wanted to ensure that no one would ever hurt him again. However, at some point, Samuel stopped trying to make excuses for their violent behavior. He knew that no matter what had happened to them, Kaseem didn't have the right to take out his demons on others.

Samuel started to pray and ask God to help him heal and get out of his wretched circumstance. He had been secretly saving money and making his plans to move. He now had enough funds to relocate somewhere and start an honest business. He didn't want to abandon his younger brothers, but his heart would no longer let him remain as Kaseem's flunky and assassin. He accepted that complying with Kaseem only enabled him to continue his destruction. The madness had to end and Kaseem's death was the only way he and the world would have peace. Therefore, he decided not to search for Kaseem or investigate his whereabouts.

Jason, the youngest of the three men, had a different attitude about Kaseem's current status. He planned to rescue his brother. He wanted to prove to Kaseem that he could handle things; and let him take a break if he needed it. Even though Jason knew there was a long list of people who wanted Kaseem dead, he never imagined life without his brother.

Jason lived in a dark, fantasy world where danger was just a concept, and gangsters were glorified as heroes. In his mind, thugs ruled the world and lived forever. He completely ignored and rejected Samuel's wisdom concerning his mindless behavior and untamed temper while he entertained his juvenile notions of invincibility.

Samuel had warned him that the morgues in big cities all over the country were overflowing with the young, dead bodies of Black men who had never been claimed. There were countless men who had died before fulfilling their potential who couldn't even be buried or cremated because there wasn't anyone who *wanted* to claim their bodies. But, Jason's twisted loyalty meant that he had to find Kaseem dead or alive and avenge his brother.

However, Jason's explosive temper and lack of critical thinking skills had doubly increased his chances of dying before his twenty-first birthday. The shrewdness that he admired in his brothers, Samuel and Kaseem is exactly what he lacked. Jason hadn't yet learned that thugs who stayed alive in the mean streets had to be smart; they had to possess the same analytical skills as other successful professionals. Most importantly, silence and taming one's tongue was often a key component to staying alive.

So, when Jason started threatening people about his brother's disappearance, he sealed and hastened his own tragic fate. As the fearful heard the news about Jason's reputation as a ruthless and unsparing street tyrant, they sought to take extreme measures to protect themselves. No one took his words lightly and soon the hunted became preoccupied with getting Jason before he destroyed them. Through ignorance and rebellion, Jason had violated one of the most important cardinal rules in war: never let your enemies know your plans.

Chapter 18
Revenge

After almost two months had passed without hearing from Kaseem, Jason became convinced that his brother was dead. Each night he tried to release his grief, but tears would never fall from his eyes. A deep sadness would try to sneak in his heart, but he kicked it before it had a chance to settle in. He told himself that he didn't have time for that kind of emotion. All he wanted to do was find Kaseem's killer or killers and make them suffer.

He refused to listen to Samuel who had tried to convince him to let things go. In fact, he no longer respected Samuel and thought he was weak for not trying to find Kaseem's killers and make them pay. He also resolved that he was not going to the police. He knew they didn't care if Kaseem was dead anyway. He was going to take matters into his own hands. And, in spite of what Samuel thought about his temper, he would be just fine.

He had made a list of people who wanted Kaseem dead. Because there were so many, he focused on people who he thought could kill his brother and get away with it. He quickly ruled out people like Mr. Townsend and some of the fake gangsters on the streets. The police were at the top of the pile, but for some reason he didn't think they were guilty this time.

His intuition kept leading him to the guy he had seen outside the courtroom after Kaseem's trial. He didn't even have the man's name, but he remembered following him because he had almost attacked Kaseem after the verdict. Jason had kept his eyes on the guy just in case he had to protect his brother. He had been telling Kaseem that he could replace Samuel as lieutenant and become his guard. He was looking for a situation to prove his loyalty and skills.

Jason suddenly remembered taping the guy talking to himself on the courthouse steps. He hoped he hadn't accidently erased it from his phone. He never forgot how menacing the guy looked even though he was dressed up. He remembered the tall, dark man praying and asking God for permission to kill Kaseem.

This greatly disturbed him for a while, but he had managed to forget that until now. With a quick Internet search about the trial, he got the guy's name: Netar Moore. He even found a photo of him and his family in one of the newspapers. He got a little excited after doing a Google search and discovered that Netar was listed as the CEO of a business on the northwest side of town.

He planned to take a few of his boys to the place and interrogate Netar when the time was right. If he didn't answer the questions right, Jason thought smiling, he was going to be praying for mercy from God instead of permission to kill his brother.

He would keep surveillance and get the guy at night when he was alone. "Yeah, his bitch momma better get her black dress out again," Jason whispered to himself.

While Netar hadn't spoken to Adara for over three months, he had kept close watch of her from a distance. Of course, she was oblivious to his presence, but he always found pleasure just looking at her. He noticed, however, that she was no longer socializing with Ivisse. He wasn't alarmed but did become curious about what happened since her co-worker was no longer coming to the library. The young woman's appearance had changed drastically, and she had started looking disheveled and stressed out.

Interestingly, he had seen Ivisse at Adara's apartment complex a few times, but he assumed she had other friends who lived there since the area was a part of the extended, college community. One day, however he realized that Ivisse had been following Adara. He also noticed that the young woman looked as if she was a few months pregnant. He had Adara's number and was tempted to call but decided to just continue to keep a close eye on things.

Adara seemed very happy as well as focused on graduating. Netar didn't want anything to upset or distract her from achieving her goal. She spent long hours at the library and Netar knew that was mainly due to her employment there. He was glad that she would graduate next month and would be leaving Atlanta. As much as he wanted to lovingly wrap his arms around her, her safety and well-being were more important to him.

The good news was that no one had reported Kaseem's disappearance to the police. Through Fitz and some of the other workers, he could get what he called *street news*. Even though those guys had given up a life of crime, they always kept their eyes and ears open to what was happening in the hood. Some of them had relatives still deeply involved in the dark underworld of crime.

125

C. Chérie Hardy

That's how Netar learned that Jason was looking for him. After work one evening Fitz said that he had something important to tell Netar. Netar appreciated that Fitz was a straightforward and honest guy who didn't feel the need to sugarcoat anything or dart around an issue. This was both his personal and business style of communication.

When Fitz entered Netar's office that night, his expression was disconcerting, and he was perspiring profusely. He sat down and immediately poured out everything he'd heard about Jason. "Netar, I hate to be the bearer of bad news, but this cat, Jason, Kaseem Jones's younger brother, is looking for you. The rumor is that he believes Kaseem is dead. Apparently, he taped you at the courthouse praying and saying you wanted to kill his brother. He's telling people that he's going to cut off your head and chop up your body in a million pieces if he finds out you killed his brother," Fitz said, it seemed without taking a breath.

"A few guys I know from my old days in the streets said that people are trying to kill Jason though. They say the guy is just as evil as Kaseem and the word is they are upset that he's threatening everybody. People describe

126

him as a ruthless monster that refuses to listen to anyone, not even his older brother Samuel who is trying to persuade him to let things go. That's why there are people planning to assassinate him before he takes someone out," he added.

"Man, this shit is crazy. That's why I am so glad I got away from that street lifestyle — nah... *death-style*. There wasn't anything I was doing that was leading to *life*. Netar, I am so glad you and your uncle gave me a chance to turn my life around. I know that I would be dead right now, just like Jason is about to be, if I hadn't met you, man," he said pausing for a long moment.

"I told some of my cousins that have heard of Jason that you are a good guy. And, that you wouldn't hurt a soul, even an evil man like Kaseem. Everyone knows people say shit that they don't mean when they're angry or hurt. Your character is solid in the streets. You've given so many brothers like me a chance in spite of our criminal record."

"Not many people would have done the same thing and we appreciate you, man. I am just telling you to stay alert because fools like Jason don't care about good people like you. Hopefully, that punk will get everything he wishes on you. I have heard that people want the whole family dead. People are so glad they don't have to deal with Kaseem's insanity that they would just take out the rest of the family in order to have peace," Fitz said.

"And, one more thing, even if you had killed Kaseem, you would have been justified. Everybody knows that sometimes killing a demon is the only way of ridding the streets of wickedness," he ended.

All Netar could do is thank Fitz for letting him know what he'd heard. He now saw Fitz as a brother and he knew he felt the same way. While he appreciated Fitz's warning, Netar did not feel afraid. He had already calculated the consequences of killing Kaseem. He knew that the risks involved one of Kaseem's brothers possibly trying to get revenge.

Netar wasn't ever going to cower in the shadows because of Jason's threats, but he was glad for the tip. The element of surprise can put a man at a disadvantage, but what only a few people knew is that he had learned how to be as lethal as the meanest of hoodlums from the gutter.

He just hoped Jason was going to bring his A-game because he was going to need it if he thought he could easily kill him. Netar didn't enjoy taking a man's life, but in self-defense he wouldn't think twice about it.

Netar didn't have to look over his shoulder though for long. One week after his talk with Fitz, two unknown men killed Jason. They decapitated his body and the young man's head would never be found. At an ungodly hour of the morning, the men disposed of Jason's truck and belongings at the same chop shop Netar had used months earlier.

When the heavily, armed guards' state-of-the-art motion sensors sounded, they cautiously watched their new visitors trying to creep down a rugged, unpaved path to their hideaway with the truck's lights turned off. Using their night vision goggles, they saw two men get out and run from the vehicle. Looking at each other, they smiled. They had not forgotten the mysterious stranger who had left them a car loaded with valuables several months ago.

As they tiptoed to the truck one man said chuckling, "Darth Vader done come back, motha fucka!"

"Damn, who is this nigga?" the other man responded, mistakenly thinking that Netar had hooked them up a second time.

"Let's see what we got tonight." While

remaining heedful and still not sure of what to expect, the men kept their guns cocked and ready to blow a hole in someone's brain. They slowly surveyed the perimeter of the truck and circumspectly opened its doors and trunk. When they could see the truck had no passengers, dead or alive, they put down their guns and started rummaging through the vehicle.

"Motha fucka, we done won Mega Millions tonight!" one man squealed when he opened a bag loaded with cash.

"Shit! I gotta talk to that nigga one day and thank his ass," the other said gleefully.

In less than an hour Jason's truck was completely stripped and untraceable. His weapons and electronic items were placed in large bins and would be later sold on the black market. Jason had now become a member of a fraternity of faceless, dead, young ruffians who no one would mourn.

In early April, a hunter discovered Jason's decomposed body in a North Georgia forest. Since the head was missing, dental records could not be used to identify him. In an effort to solve the case, the police released the story to all the major news stations in Atlanta. In addition to clothing, they described two pieces of unique jewelry found at the crime scene.

The first was a large, gold ring with a snake's head carved in middle. Rubies were used for the eyes and a diamond was located in the reptile's mouth. The second article would cause the discovery to be added to the book of urban legends. It was a simple, cross necklace with the name, Gitele Moore engraved vertically on the back. "We love you" was also on the back written horizontally to intersect the two phrases.

Once the descriptions of the jewelry and articles of clothing were published, the media frenzy resumed after hearing Gitele Moore's name. The eerie discovery had directly connected Kaseem Jones to her murder for a second time. Her name echoed across the radio and television waves like she was a ghost screaming for justice beyond the grave.

The police contacted the Moore family to verify ownership of the necklace. With tears in her eyes, Netar's mother did her only television interview and explained that she and her husband had the necklace custom-made for Gitele's sixteenth birthday. When they had not found the precious keepsake after the trial, they had prayed that one day it would be returned to them. While the news outlets begged to hear more from the family, the discovery of the necklace had re-opened so many painful wounds.

Members of Gitele's family declined doing interviews and asked that the media respect their privacy and time of grief. Netar returned to New York to be with his parents and brother while the investigation continued in Atlanta. He knew his presence would give everyone greater peace of mind.

The police also asked Samuel Jones, the only surviving brother of his notorious clan, to reveal the identity of the headless body. Expressionless and without hesitation, he announced that the clothing and ring belonged to his brother, Kaseem. He was relieved that no one challenged his response; and, not a soul from the media ever mentioned Jason Jones's name.

Samuel believed that he would finally have peace with both of his bloodthirsty brothers dead. He was going to leave his checkered past and start anew. However, before saying "adieu" to all he had ever known, there was one thing he wanted to do. He just couldn't leave town without thanking Mr. Townsend for his example and effort to teach him right from wrong. Samuel also knew that he had to be quick and discreet because if he was ever caught in his old neighborhood again, he would probably share his siblings' fate. He had witnessed countless times people die because of their association. He knew people wanted his entire family erased from the planet.

Packing nothing, he headed to Mr. Townsend's apartment on foot. As he passed some of the familiar faces, he could see the gloating in their eyes. Their joy from Kaseem's demise was undeniable. Most of them knew that Jason was also dead. It seemed the people he passed telepathically communicated that they wanted him dead, too. He could feel their hatred and he couldn't even blame them for it.

Praying Mr. Townsend would allow him to enter his home, he ran up the stairs as fast as he could. The old man seemed to open the door before he had knocked. It was as if he had been expecting him. "Good afternoon, Mr. Townsend," Samuel started.

"Come on in, young man. Have a seat," Mr. Townsend said pleasantly. "Could I get you something to drink?"

"No thank you, sir. I can only stay for a few minutes. I am about to leave town, but I wanted to tell you how much I really appreciate you. I never forgot how you used to try to teach the boys in the neighborhood how to do right. You set a good example for us and I know most of those guys were too young and foolish to realize it at the time, but you were just trying to show you cared. Because of you, Mr. Townsend, I know how to live as a man with integrity," Samuel said.

Mr. Townsend smiled as Samuel continued, "I also want to say I am very sorry about what Kaseem did to you and your wife. It was wrong. And, I was wrong for not stopping him and I want to ask for your forgiveness for that, sir," Samuel ended with his head hung down with humility.

"I forgive you, son. I know you put that money in my mailbox. I have been watching and praying for you many years. I know you were the only boy paying attention to me when you were younger. You never threw those rocks at me and God protected you for that. All of your brothers and sister are dead, but you're alive because God wants to do an amazing work in your life," Mr. Townsend said.

The elderly man rested his voice for a minute and continued, "I am not perfect and when I was younger, I didn't always do what I should have. But, I thank the Lord that He had mercy on me. What I was trying to be for you young men, was exactly what someone was to me. That's how I learned how to do things differently. A righteous man taught me. Go now and be safe. I love you, but God loves you more," he said with his voice trembling with emotion.

As Samuel and Mr. Townsend hugged, the elderly man said a quiet prayer. Samuel was going to need it because a group of young, homicidal men were already waiting for him outside. They hadn't just planned to kill Samuel, they salivated thinking about torturing him. Their fear of the Joneses had dissipated with the knowledge that Kaseem and Jason were dead.

However, through divine guidance, Mr. Townsend ushered Samuel to his back door and told him to leave as quietly as he could. He advised him not to ever return to his home for his own safety and that he would keep him in his prayers.

Samuel Jones vanished in the night defying many odds. He was twenty-eight years old and had never been shot or stabbed. He was richer than the average human being in the world. He was sane in spite of all the insanity he had experienced and committed. He believed that God still loved him. He knew that God had a good plan for him and that's why He had protected him throughout the years. God had removed his enemies, even those who lurked in his own family.

Samuel decided that he would strive to be like Mr. Townsend to his own children and anybody else he would meet in the future. He had a peace that surpassed all understanding. As he sat on a plane heading for Ohio, he smiled and looked out the window. He relaxed and rejoiced that his heart was as high from God's grace, as his body was safely flying in the sky.

Chapter 19
News

News about the discovery of Gitele's necklace, and Kaseem's headless body, rapidly started swirling around Hilliard University's campus. Gitele had once been a beautiful, honor student with a bright future, and many professors decided her tragic story was just too big and important not to discuss. Their primary goal was to generate more awareness about domestic violence, particularly among young people.

When Ivisse learned about Kaseem's fate as she sat in class one afternoon, she nearly fainted. She was about five months pregnant and clearly showing. Struggling to hold back a volcanic eruption of emotions, she quietly excused herself from class and began walking to her dorm room as fast as she could.

Several classmates became concerned as she rushed pass them with tears streaming down her face. Grateful that she didn't have a roommate, Ivisse let her emotions flow uninhibited for several hours. While she felt a bit of relief from finally knowing what had happened to her beloved, it hurt to hear his name sullied in the media.

Everyone was labeling Kaseem a monster, but she had recognized so many good things about him. At some point, she realized that she was the only person to ever love Kaseem unconditionally. As she lied on her bed and she stroked abdomen softly, she remembered his gentle hands touching her. She trembled as she reminisced about how good their intimate moments had been. She hated that she would no longer feel his masculine embrace. She felt devastated that Kaseem would not be around to raise their son. She decided at that moment to do whatever it took to protect her child from the vicious lies about his father.

Ivisse was also relieved to now know that Adara didn't have any involvement in Kaseem's disappearance or death. She hadn't seen Adara since the day she quit her job at the library. Regretfully, due to her fragile, crazed mental state, Ivisse had cursed out Adara and Ms. Cooper before storming out of the building.

Her jealousy of her friend had distorted her thinking and she had been following Adara for months. But today with the truth finally revealed, she concluded the card and letter she had found in her purse were probably not from Kaseem. After all, both items had been unsigned. She felt a cloud of shame engulf her as she recalled how she had treated her friend. Adara had been the only classmate at Hilliard to demonstrate how much she genuinely cared for her.

Moreover, it was such a relief to stop stalking her one, true friend. Ivisse had barely been able to keep up her studies while hoping she'd get a sighting of Kaseem at Adara's apartment. All this time he had been dead and no doubt from foul play. Imagining his decapitated body made her start crying again. She couldn't fathom how people could be so barbaric.

Ivisse rationalized that even if Kaseem had Gitele's necklace it didn't prove that he had killed her. However, every time she had that thought, she also had to override the nagging, sick feeling that Kaseem *was* guilty of murder.

Denying the truth was the only way she could preserve her sanity. Deep within the core of her heart she knew that she trivialized her late lover's evil in order not to hate herself. The idea that she had fallen in love with a coldblooded killer would have destroyed her.

C. Chérie Hardy

With Kaseem's reputation being reported in the news, she would not share the identity of her child's father. It would be a secret she would take to her grave. She hadn't even told her parents she was pregnant, but they would find out in a few weeks when they arrived to Atlanta for her graduation. She would just have to figure out a way to dodge their questions. It was too late to have an abortion anyway, even if her parents tried to demand it.

Ivisse just hoped her baby's health was okay. She had been stressed out during the first trimester, but now with some closure concerning Kaseem, she hoped she would feel better. She decided to schedule an appointment with the clinic for prenatal care and resolved to take better care of herself.

She would also write Adara a long letter apologizing and explaining her shameful behavior. All of her old thoughts of unjustified revenge had dried up inside her. She hoped her friend would forgive her and that they could patch things up. She really missed their talks and Adara's sunny disposition. If they didn't rekindle their friendship before graduation, Ivisse would probably never see or talk to Adara again. This saddened her because she wanted

Adara to be her child's godmother.

Ivisse would also write Ms. Cooper at the library. Ms. Cooper had really tried to help her, but her temporary insanity could not be penetrated. The old woman hadn't deserved to be disrespected. She was one of the nicest people Ivisse had ever known. She had to find a way to demonstrate to her mentor how remorseful she was.

That weekend Ivisse implemented her plan of action to make amends with the people in her life. She told herself that God didn't make mistakes. Everything she had endured, whether self-imposed or otherwise, served a purpose in her life.

She made up her mind that she would find the silver lining in her depressing situation and become a mother that her son would admire, love and respect. And, most importantly, she would raise her son with the fear and admonition of the Lord. He would honor God and atone for his father's transgressions.

Chapter 20
Graduation

Because Adara didn't have a television, she had not been able to watch the news. Fortunately, she heard about Kaseem's death through Ms. Cooper at the library. While she knew the real story, she was glad about what had been reported in the media. She hoped this meant that she and Netar could finally be together without the threat of danger skulking in the shadows of their lives.

However, although the story broke weeks ago, she still hadn't heard from Netar. There were countless times when she wanted to pick up the phone and call, but he had ordered her to do so only if she was facing a life-threatening situation. She remembered he'd said he would contact her once he felt that the coast was clear.

With graduation just a few days away, she was starting to wonder if Netar's feelings had changed. She thought of a thousand reasons why he wouldn't want her. She had never believed she was good enough for a man in his league anyway.

She couldn't imagine what he could find attractive about a poor, country bumpkin like her. While some people would call that kind of thinking spiritually damaging or self-deprecating, she considered it honesty. Adara believed that the only way she could protect her heart was by facing the truth, no matter how harsh it turned out to be. Besides, she told herself while trying not to shed tears, if he really cared, he would have contacted her by now. He would have made an effort to see her graduate she thought.

Sometimes she allowed herself to fantasize about him suddenly appearing with his winsome smile and cradling her in his arms. On the other hand, she cautioned herself that any kind of emotional indulgence involving Netar would only hurt her more in the long run.

Her grandmother had taught her that a man's actions always spoke louder than his words. "You never have to guess what a man is thinking; you don't have wonder if he likes you. A man acts according to what's in his heart. And, if you're on his mind, he'll let you know," she'd often say. Well, Netar was shouting his feelings through space, Adara lamented as she endured the sting of rejection.

The good news was that she and Ivisse had reconciled their friendship. Although Adara couldn't share details of her personal experience with Netar, she was relieved to have someone who could relate to her general philosophy about things; someone who would find her wry jokes comical. She was also comforted knowing that Ivisse's mental and physical health had greatly improved. Additionally, Adara was ecstatic about being the child's godmother. She had vowed to keep the child's father's identity a secret.

Thankfully, planning for the baby's future became a welcomed distraction to Adara's thoughts about Netar. Ivisse had decided to name the baby, Dirk which meant "leader" in Scandinavian. She and Adara joked about not knowing any African-American men with the name which they rationalized made it even more suitable for the child.

The two young women also created positive affirmations and confessions to speak over the boy's life. Ivisse now felt more comfortable openly talking about Kaseem's reputation and no longer seemed hyper-sensitive about his past. She declared that with love, her son's life would be the antithesis of his father's.

On graduation day, Adara and Ivisse

reflected on how much they had endured together. Their friendship had been purified with fire. Ivisse's parents seemed to take the news about their daughter's pregnancy better than anticipated. This made the graduate beam with joy. She had already started to glow now that so many issues had been resolved in her life.

Before leaving campus for the last time, Adara searched the crowd hoping to see Netar standing somewhere in the distance. She had clung to a remnant of hope that his delay in contacting her was due to some unforeseen problem that she didn't know about. The spotlight had recently been on him and his family after the discovery of his sister's necklace.

She reasoned that perhaps Netar was trying to preserve her privacy and safety by keeping her in the shadows. Perhaps once the news had become old, he would remind her how special she was to him. His physical absence from this special moment, only mentally heightened her sense of longing for him, but she just couldn't stop the myriad of conflicting thoughts that continued to jumble around in her mind.

When Adara returned to her apartment that day, she took out the love letter that Netar

C. Chérie Hardy

had given her for Christmas. At some point she had forced herself to stop reading it because the more she did, the harder it was to stop reminiscing about Netar. She decided to indulge herself one last time before discarding it.

My dearest Adara,
How could I fully articulate my love for you, ma chérie? It's immeasurable, unconquerable, unconditional, incorruptible, infinite... No adjective in all the languages of the world could adequately describe the depth, purity and sincerity of what I feel for you.

Some nights I can't even sleep from being so awed that God allowed our paths to cross in such an unexpected and amazing way. Adara, you are, and have everything, I've ever desired in a woman. I'm still surprised to discover that you really exist! You are more special to me than my most beautiful dreams and hopes for a helpmate. You are like a rare, perfect gemstone – priceless. You are so valuable to me that nothing could compensate for your worth.

Adara, please know that I never want to live in this world without you beside me. Just like God made Eve for Adam, He made you for me. I know that as one, we will do great things for the Lord. Ma chérie, you bring out the best in me. I often smile and rejoice knowing that our heartbeats do a dance ensemble of moves as the music of love swirls within us.

Three Nights in December

Adara, ma chérie adorable et spéciale, please let me love you until I take my final breath. Of all the gifts God has bestowed upon me, you are the one I cherish the most. I see you as a blessing, and I cannot thank God enough for you.

Mon amour, never forget that while the Master Potter of the universe created you to be respected, loved and admired by many, you were made to be held by me alone.

Finalement, tu es mon addiction. J'ai besoin de toi toujours. Je t'adore, ma chérie. Je suis à toi.

Ton amour.

In spite of the letter filled with Netar's declarations of his love and devotion, Adara's heart sank with sadness. Fighting off tears, she threw the letter away after she had torn it into tiny pieces. Then, using all of her mental, emotional and spiritual strength, she tried to focus on how blessed she was to be getting a college degree without student loans, and having the job of her dreams waiting for her back home. She pleaded with God to help her move forward as well as heal her broken heart. She reminded herself that she possessed a countless number of things for which to be grateful and vowed not to ever meditate on what she never really had.

C. Chérie Hardy

While it was difficult, she finally accepted that she had been dreaming and now was awakened to the harsh reality that Netar had never really loved her. She scolded herself inwardly for how easily she had believed his lies. She suddenly remembered all the red flags she'd missed concerning their incompatibility.

She also felt embarrassed thinking how he must be joking about her to all his friends. They must have been on the floor almost dying from laughter when he told them about how she wanted to be a nun. Adara sometimes cringed thinking how she almost gave her body to man who probably saw her as a stupid, unsophisticated, school girl from the backwoods of North Carolina. But, she gave him credit for sparing her more shame by not accepting her virginity.

As she headed home the day following graduation, Adara prayed again that God would erase the three nights of memories she had created with Netar. It didn't make sense for such a brief span of time to have such a powerful effect on her life. She fervently hoped that eventually the images she cherished of Netar would fade and the pangs of rejection and loss would lessen with time.

Chapter 21
The Gift

Adara was learning that time didn't heal all wounds; it only made them more endurable. It had been almost nine months since she's heard from Netar and she had finally come to a place of peace. She chose to spend her time expressing gratitude for the abundant blessings she had instead of fretting about the things and people that were no longer in her life. She knew that it was possible to live without Netar because she already had. And while she regularly prayed for the health of his body, mind and spirit, she had mentally released him and the hope that they would ever reunite.

The old cliché, "What is meant to be will be" helped her to accept the outcome of any situation. She believed that through God's amazing love she'd have what she needed, and the things she didn't, He'd take away. Her job was to align her desires with His perfect will and continue to live in a way that was pleasing to Him.

Adara was especially appreciative of her work as an educator. She enjoyed the productive busyness and constantly sought out innovative and challenging ways to empower her students. And, although she used so much of herself to inspire them, the satisfaction and spiritual fulfillment she gained was worth every second of her time and energy.

She had taken a maieutic, instructional approach to bringing out the best in her students, and every day she became encouraged by their creativity, inquisitiveness and passion for learning. She often wished that she could have more hours in a day to help navigate their learning. The added bonus was that her experiences as a teacher kept her mind focused on reality rather than pipe dreams.

The Christmas season had come again and Adara was excited about her students' community service projects. She had instilled in them that one of the most important things in life was devoting their time and gifts to others, especially the less fortunate. During the week before the holiday vacation, she had arranged volunteer opportunities for them. She couldn't have been happier and prouder when all of them kept their commitments to the needy families who were counting on them.

As Adara prepared to go on her two-week break, she kept thinking it would be the

Three Nights in December

first Christmas without her beloved grandmother who had passed away a few months
after her graduation. Adara later discovered that
the selfless woman who raised her had fought
hard to stay alive until she finished college. This
sacrifice had left an indelible mark on her heart.
She would terribly miss her beloved, but she
was comforted knowing that her spirit was in
eternal quiescence with God.

Adara had concluded that nothing erased
memories except disease and death. Memories
didn't magically evaporate no matter how hard
or long we prayed. No, God didn't remove
them, He healed them. He used them to teach
people lessons. He used them to make us
stronger, wiser, and humbler That's how people
learned to keep living even when their beloved
had gone away.

The unconditional love Adara's
grandmother had given her was more powerful
than death. It would remain in her heart forever;
it was a gift she'd have to give away to others in
spite of her pain. She was immensely grateful for
the limited time she'd had with such a beautiful
person.

As a way to cope with the devastating
loss, she decided to move to a small, neighboring

town that was only a fifteen-minute drive from the school where she worked. She hadn't been ready to leave her childhood home, but it was the only way she could manage her grief. Her new abode was a quaint, ranch-style home with two bedrooms, two full bathrooms, and a large kitchen and living room. She had gotten the extra space so that Ivisse and Dirk could enjoy a second home on the East Coast whenever they visited.

On Friday evening after work Adara finished her Christmas shopping for Ivisse and Dirk. She wished that they could visit for the holiday, but it was too cold, and the child was too young to fly across the country. Each time Adara passed the picture of her two, favorite people she smiled and said a prayer for her godson. She professed that he would become an agent of God in spite of Kaseem's DNA in his blood. Adara believed that God superseded history and genetics. Dirk's future would not be doomed because of his biological connections.

After showering, she made a cup of hot, green tea, and curled up on her sofa to finish reading J. California Cooper's book, *The Wake of the Wind*. She hadn't been able to put the book down for days. While her house was warm and toasty, she wished she had learned how to use the fireplace. Several people had explained what to do, but she still felt a bit apprehensive. The thought of reading by firelight seemed nice, but she didn't like the idea of dealing with smoke and fire.

She hadn't put up a Christmas tree, but had placed a few decorative, holiday figurines on her end-tables and fireplace mantle. The scent of fresh pine and her homemade potpourri permeated around the house.

Many women her age might have felt depressed on a Friday night without a mate or even a prospect of a date, but she didn't. As an only child, growing up in a home with *a seasoned saint*, she had learned to appreciate and prefer solitude. She particularly enjoyed reading without distractions in a tranquil space. It was one of her most favorite, leisurely things to do.

Eventually, she fell asleep with her book in her lap, but was jolted awake when her doorbell rang. She glanced at a clock; it was after midnight. Immediately, her heart began to race. She feared that someone was going to bring her more bad news.

C. Chérie Hardy

Who could it be this time? Please God, not Ivisse or Dirk! Not her aunt or nephews. I can't bear another loss right now, Lord!

Taking a deep breath she said, "Who is it?" while trying to peek unnoticed through the blinds of her front door's side panels. For some reason her porch light sensor wasn't working and she couldn't see much in the thick darkness.

"It's Netar," she heard.

"Excuse me?"

"Adara, it is Netar Moore," he answered.

"Just a moment," Adara said breathlessly. "Let me grab something decent to put on." As she walked to her bedroom to put on her classic, oversized shirt and sweat pants, she tried to stop her heart from racing. She still couldn't believe that it was Netar standing outside her front door.

She looked through one of the door's side panel again and quickly recognized the familiar, large silhouette of Netar's body. Without the porch light working, the only thing she could see clearly was the large, gold, gift bag he was holding.

Adara slowly opened the door. As Netar entered the living room his eyes hungrily looked over Adara who gestured for him to sit on the loveseat as she moved to the sofa a few feet away. Immediately, he felt he had entered an ethereal realm. It felt so good to be in Adara's presence that his body warmed up with passion.

Several moments of clamorous silence lingered in the air as their spirits conversed without words. Netar unabashedly searched Adara's face and thought she was love personified. In his mind, she was a personalized gift from Heaven. He saw her as a spiritual conduit through whom the love of God flowed. His heart told God again that he would cherish and protect this blessing for the rest of his life.

Adara sat stoically, not ready to meet Netar's gaze. She couldn't believe the man she had tried so arduously to forget was sitting in her living room, appearing like an Adonis wearing a black, heavy, turtleneck sweater, a leather jacket and jeans. The scent of his body, cologne and leather wafted around the room and assaulted her with memories of their intimacy.

Netar knew that Adara's reaction was a result of her hurt and disappointment from their lack of communication, but he wanted her to know that she had been a part of his thoughts from his first glimpse of her. Because he couldn't risk her safety, he had attended her graduation and even her grandmother's funeral incognito.

She would never know how much it broke his heart that he could not share those moments with her in his arms. However, he had returned trying to make up for all the time they'd missed. He now felt certain that Samuel and the police had completely closed Kaseem's murder case. The moment had finally come when he could safely be with Adara up close and personal rather than afar.

Adara, on the other hand, braced herself for whatever explanation Netar was going to give for his prolonged disappearance. No matter how hard it might be, she was not going to run into his arms as if she'd forgotten about him missing her graduation and failing to check on her well-being. He didn't owe her anything, but because of his broken promises, she had placed an impermeable gate around her heart. Netar, nor any other man, would have the key to enter it.

Netar finally broke the silence. "Adara, I hope you will forgive me for not doing this sooner. You may not believe this, but I wanted to make sure you would be safe before I resumed our relationship. Ma chérie, I love you. I have thought of you for the last 412 days of my life," he said.

Three Nights in December

"That even includes the days before we had ever met. I hope you will accept my apology and my hand in marriage," he added.

Adara desperately wanted to believe Netar. The three nights she had spent with him had irreversibly changed her life. The love she felt for him was in every molecule of her body and would only die when she did. However, despite her feelings, she wouldn't just open her heart so easily. The pain of getting hurt again was too much to bear.

"Netar, I would be lying if I didn't say that you haven't been in my thoughts and prayers since the moment we met, but when I didn't hear from you; when you missed my graduation; and even my grandmother's funeral, I couldn't determine how you really felt about me," Adara shared calmly.

"I am not ashamed to say that I love you, but your actions told me that I was insignificant to you. How could I have misinterpreted them? If you had just hinted in some small way that you cared, maybe I could trust you right now," Adara said with emotion swelling in her voice.

She continued, "Netar, it's hard to believe a man could love a woman who he doesn't speak to for nine months. You will never know how much I needed you when my grandmother died. I thank you for being concerned about my safety, but did you have to completely abandon me?"

Netar slowly reached into the bag and took out a red envelope and handed it to Adara. When she gave him a puzzled look, he said, "Open it. This is one your Christmas gifts."

Adara stared in astonishment at the first picture that she removed from the envelope. Things didn't mentally register instantly when she saw herself, Ivisse and their family members after their Hilliard graduation ceremony. It took a moment to realize that Netar had photographed them. There were several other photos, too. She found images that he had taken of her and her small family at her grandmother's graveside service.

"Netar, you were there? You had not forgotten me?" she asked softly with her voice brimming with emotion.

Netar wrapped his arms around Adara as a gallon of tears poured from her eyes. "Here, take my phone and you'll find more pictures there, too. I don't want there to ever be any doubt about how much I love you," Netar whispered in her ears.

Three Nights in December

Adara looked through his phone and saw hundreds of photos that he had taken. There were several dated before they had ever met. When Adara looked at him questioningly he said, "Yes, I took some of those while Kaseem was hunting you. I have looked at every photo, every day since the first moment I saw you."

"Thank you, Netar," she said humbly. "Forgive me for not trusting you — for not believing you'd keep your promises."

Adara's voice sounded so sweet to Netar. He had often longed to hear it during their separation. He gently embraced his future wife and said, "You're welcome, my angel. Je t'aime toujours, ma chérie adorable." Then he slowly kneeled while holding one of Adara's warm, soft hands. He took out a ring that he had custommade for her. It was a three-carat, heart-shaped onyx surrounded by diamonds.

"Adara Emelle Jacobson, would you please bless and honor me, angel, by allowing me to be in your life as your husband until I take my last breath?" Netar said.

Adara managed to sputter her affirmative response before she and Netar shared a long, ardent kiss.

Acknowledgements

Heavenly Father,
I thank you for spiritually infecting me with "writing fever". Writing has been one of the most cathartic and therapeutic activities I've done over the years and I am immensely grateful that You have allowed me to accomplish one of my long-term goals — complete a novel. What could I do without you, Lord? Absolutely nothing! So, I thank You for being my faithful Rod and Staff.

Felicia,
For the past 24 years, I've been blessed to call you "daughter". I love how you "keep it real" yet encourage me to pursue my dreams. I cherish your honest feedback and thank you for being my most enthusiastic cheerleader. I am on "Team Felicia" always! Much love, dear.

Yolanda,
While I've desired to pen a novel since my youth, it was your inspiration and wisdom that helped to propel me to this moment. Without your encouragement, I probably would have put this off for another ten years. Thank you so much!

Acknowledgements

Tiffany and Aleatha,
You have patiently read all the books I've written over the years and managed to stay positive about my efforts. I am grateful for your time and support in all my endeavors.

Suzanne Horwitz,
I appreciate you creating an awesome book cover. Your patience, professionalism, and sincere desire to help others are what make you stand out. I am so grateful to have you on my team.

Jameka Fields,
Your suggestions and insight have added so much value to this book. I sincerely appreciate your feedback. Be fabulous on purpose!

To my favorite author, J. California Cooper,
Thank you for creating good literature for the world to read! I have not only been entertained but educated about so many aspects of life through your awesome books! My prayer is that future generations of readers will discover your literary treasures!

About the Author

C. Chérie Hardy was born and raised in Florida. She is an award-winning educator and inspirational speaker. She has taught world languages as well as world literature for 30 years.

While *Three Nights in December* is her first novel, Hardy is the author of several books for children including *The Orange Zebra, This Beautiful Hair of Mine* and *Princess Valerie: A Story About Generosity and Service*. In 2003, she published the first edition of *Love Doesn't Hurt: Life Lessons for Young Women* and *Wise and Wonderful: Life Lessons for Single Mothers (as C. Chérie Brown)*. She is also the author of *Daily Pearls: 365 Inspirational Quotes and Scriptures; The Power of Gratitude: 365 Quotes and Scriptures for Healing Your Mind, Body, and Heart; and Encouragement for the Grieving Heart: 365 Uplifting Quotes and Scriptures for Coping with Loss.*

C. Chérie Hardy is the proud parent of one daughter. She currently resides with her family in the Atlanta metropolitan area. You can send your questions and comments to her at: **ccheriehardy@gmail.com**

Notes

Connect with Avant-garde Books!

Mailing Address:
Post Office Box 566
Mableton, Georgia 30126

Website:
www.avantgardebooks.net

Facebook:
@avantgardebooks100

Twitter:
@Avant_GardeBks

Instagram:
@Avantgardebooks

Email:
avantgardebooks@gmail.com

www.ingramcontent.com/pod-product-compliance
Lightning Source LLC
Chambersburg PA
CBHW032012170626
46807CB00006B/2771